AUTHOR	CLASS
PENTECOST, H.	AFC

TITLE Walking dead man
Large print edition

WALKING DEAD MAN

George Battle, the second richest man in the world and the owner of the plush Hotel Beaumont, had just escaped getting a bullet in his forehead whilst he was asleep. But how could the would-be killer know that Mr Battle would be in the penthouse that night and not its rightful occupant, the hotel manager, Pierre Chambrun? Despite warnings that he was the intended victim, Chambrun insisted on conducting a search for the unknown gunman. Then Chambrun himself disappeared . . .

HUGH PENTECOST

WALKING DEAD MAN

Complete and Unabridged

LINFORD
Leicester

First published in the
United States of America

First Linford Edition
published 1997

British Library CIP Data

Pentecost, Hugh, *1903*–
    Walking dead man.—Large print ed.—
Linford mystery library
1. Detective and mystery stories
2. Large type books
I. Title
813.5′2 [F]

ISBN 0–7089–5158–9

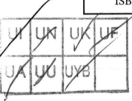

07245918

Published by
F. A. Thorpe (Publishing) Ltd.
Anstey, Leicestershire

Set by Words & Graphics Ltd.
Anstey, Leicestershire
Printed and bound in Great Britain by
T. J. International Ltd., Padstow, Cornwall

This book is printed on acid-free paper

Part One

1

IT started out like a comedy. It didn't end that way.

Both groups arrived in the late afternoon of the same day, like rival traveling circuses, each trumpeting its presence. Part of the comedy was that I had been warned, as public relations man for the Hotel Beaumont, that neither group wanted its presence known. They were to be gotten, unnoticed and unsung, to their various suites. There would be no stopping at the main desk to register. They were to be anonymous. I had no reason to believe that the two groups were in any way connected. It developed that they were connected by about seven million dollars which, as the fellow said, ain't hay.

The first group, the one that concerned me most, was symbolic of money, huge

3

quantities of money. Mr. George Battle, owner of the Hotel Beaumont, who hadn't been in the United States for seventeen years, claimed, modestly, that he was only the second richest man in the world. The second group was symbolic of romance, which is a polite word for sex. David Loring, the film star, also modest, admitted that a great many women said he was the greatest lover of all time, but that he laid claim to no title, since in thirty-five years of living and loving he hadn't been able to cover the entire field. He said, smiling that devastatingly slow smile of his, that he needed a little more time before he could conscientiously accept the championship. Those women who do not resent being considered sex objects were willing to crown him king without waiting for any more field work. One of them fainted dead away at the mere sight of David when he stepped out of a cream-colored Continental limousine at ten minutes to four that afternoon.

He was preceded into the Beaumont's lobby by a dwarf. This one had a large and strangely beautiful head. He had dark hair, worn rather long, limpid brown eyes wide with mischief, and a neatly trimmed Vandyke beard and mustache. That head belonged to a laughing Mephistopheles. The body was the cruelly twisted frame of a crippled child. He was not quite four feet tall. He skipped and danced ahead of the golden sex king, who followed, modestly, a gorgeous brunette in a black see-through dress clinging to his arm. Following them were thirty-six suitcases and attaché cases carried by the Beaumont's bell corps. Bringing up the rear were two men completely overlooked by the panting ladies in the lobby. One of them was the slim, dark, intense Maxie Zorn, who had made it from the garment district to top independent film producer in Hollywood in the first forty years of his life. He is now Maxwell Zorn on the theater marquees. The second man was a blond, almost crew cut, which is out of style these days, wearing a grey herringbone tweed jacket on a football player's back and shoulders. He had a tight, hard mouth and his face was made expressionless by wire-rimmed black glasses. I found out later he was Richard Cleaves, novelist and writer of David Loring's upcoming epic. The 'epic' was getting a lot of press coverage because Maxie Zorn had shrewdly announced that he was still searching for just the right girl to appear in a seven-minute segment of the film in bed with David, both stark naked. Naturally the 'epic' would be X-rated. Unnoticed, unsung? Brother! Women seemed to have appeared out of the woodwork, and David stood in the center of a panting mob, looking boyish, helpless, and oh so male.

It was a fascinating spectacle and I could have watched it forever, but I was ripped away from it by Johnny Thacker, the day bell captain.

"The Man," he told me, "is just

arriving at the side entrance."

Mr. George Battle was my job, and I elbowed my way through the crowd and headed for the side entrance. Unnoticed and unsung? There were two huge black Cadillacs at the door. The second one was empty except for the chauffeur. There seemed to be a great many people trying to get out of the first one. There was a dark young man with bulging muscles wearing a tight-fitting jacket that wasn't tailored to hide the gun he was carrying in a shoulder holster. He was followed by a monstrously fat old man, wheezing and gasping for breath, a cigarette dangling from flabby lips, his watery eyes narrowed against the late afternoon sun. Then came a man in a black suit and wearing a black bowler who had 'manservant' written all over him. He looked like a middle-aged Melville Cooper. The three men looked at the outer façade of the Beaumont as though they had all arrived at the wrong place.

And then Shelda came out of the car.

Shelda Mason is a long story which will get gradually told, but let me say here that I had been so much in love with her and so close to her that I could feel my gut ache just looking at her. I hadn't seen her for a year. I knew she was coming with Battle. I thought I was prepared. It was all over between us and it would be no problem to say a casual hello. I was wrong. It was a problem. My mouth felt full of dust.

"Hello, Mark," she said in her low, throaty voice.

"Hi," I said. She turned to the manservant. "Allerton, this is Mr. Haskell, the public relations man for the hotel."

"Howjudoo," Allerton said, very British.

"Where's Chambrun?" the guntoter asked.

"This is Ed Butler, Mr. Battle's bodyguard," Shelda said. "And Dr.

Cobb, Mr. Battle's personal physician." I could have sworn she was fighting a little twitch at the corner of her mouth. She wanted to laugh.

"Mr. Chambrun is waiting for you in the penthouse," I said. "I'm to take you all there."

Butler turned to the car and opened the rear door. What came out was a tall, very thin man completely hidden inside a loose-fitting black overcoat with a mink collar. The collar was turned up and the brim of a black fedora was pulled down so that all I could see of his face were two very bright blue eyes. He looked furtively up and down the sidewalk.

"Okay, Buster, lead the way," the bodyguard said.

We went through the revolving door and were instantly inundated by the clammering and yammering from the main lobby.

"Oh, God!" I heard a voice say. It was Battle's.

"What the hell's going on in there?"

the bodyguard asked. A brown hand caressed the bulge in his jacket as though, I thought, he had hopes of using the gun.

"David Loring and a bevy of admirers," I said.

"How do we get through them without being seen?"

"You don't," I said.

"You better effing well find a way," he said.

He said 'effing'. I didn't clean it up.

"Language, Edward, language!" Dr. Cobb wheezed, and then indulged in a kind of shuddering, noiseless laughter.

"The service elevator from the ballroom?" Shelda suggested. She was thinking, bless her. She had once been my secretary. She knew the hotel as well as I did.

The bodyguard looked at Dr. Cobb as if he was measuring him for a coffin. Then he said to me: "So move!"

The side entrance to the ballroom was only a couple of yards away and

I led the parade into the great, empty elegance, through a service pantry, and to the undecorated service elevator. We could all get in it without any problem. Mr. Battle stayed hidden behind his mink collar and his hat. We started up.

I glanced at Shelda. She was looking demurely down at the toe of a calfskin pump. I wondered whose bed she'd been sharing for the last year. I wondered if she was wondering the same thing about me.

★ ★ ★

One thing that puzzled me about Mr. Battle's visit to the Beaumont was what had been arranged to accommodate him and his staff for a week's stay. The Beaumont is the world's top luxury hotel. It contains a dozen of the world's most elegant suites. There are two fancy duplexes. In addition to its hundreds of rooms and suites for transient guests there are ten cooperatively owned apartments on the top two floors and three cooperatively owned penthouses on the roof. These apartments and penthouses were serviced by the hotel but owned by the tenants. One of these penthouses belongs to Pierre Chambrun, the legendary manager of the Beaumont. Since these penthouses cost about a quarter of a million dollars on the open market, you would have to guess that Chambrun was a very wealthy man. I happen to know that his salary is in the neighborhood of $50,000 a year, but that he came to this country, penniless, after World War II. It would have been difficult for him to accumulate the kind of capital that would buy him the penthouse. The fact of the matter was that it had been a gift from the owner, Mr. George Battle. At some point in their relationship Chambrun, who was indispensable to the operation of the hotel, had threatened to quit.

What the quarrel was about I don't know, but in the end Battle deeded over the penthouse to his indispensable man. Chambrun stayed on, and someone had remarked that if Battle ever decided to fire him, Chambrun would still be there, pouring sand in the machinery if anyone dared to take over from him.

Chambrun is a short, dark, square little man with black eyes buried in deep pouches. Those eyes can be compassionately warm or cold as a hanging judge's. The hotel is like a small city, with its own shops, its own restaurants and bars, its own hospital, gymnasium, bank stores. It has its own police department. It is the home-away-from-home for scores of foreign diplomats in New York on United Nations business. The staff, in every department, is expert and trained by Chambrun himself. He presides over the entire operation with some kind of psychic radar awareness of everything that is going on in every nook and cranny of the enterprise. Over the years one or two new employees have imagined that they could get away with something behind Chambrun's back. The speed with which the boom was lowered in those cases was a lesson to all of us. Loyalty is the key to Chambrun's success — loyalty out of love and regard for him or fear of him. Either way it works. You can reach him at any time, day or night, if you have a problem, and if you try to solve the problems without him, he somehow knows about it and comes to you.

I have been working for Chambrun for about eight years and I have only been in the penthouse twice. It is the place to which he retreats; where he lives whatever his private life may be. That is why we all wondered why Chambrun had evacuated his penthouse so that Mr. George Battle could live there during his stay. I had asked Miss Ruysdale, Chambrun's fabulous secretary, about it. Miss Ruysdale is a handsome, beautifully turned-out woman in her mid-thirties. She has her own office just outside

Chambrun's on the second floor. She protects him from unnecessary irritations, appears to read his mind, and there is gossip that she may very well take care of much more personal needs. She's very special, an original. He calls her Ruysdale — never Betsy or Miss Ruysdale. Only once, when he thought she was in danger, have I seen him be anything but impersonal about her. And yet we wondered about them.

"What do you know about Mr. Battle?" Miss Ruysdale asked when I questioned her about the penthouse arrangement.

"That he lives on the French Riviera, counting his money," I said. "In a chateau surrounded by a high wall with an electrified fence."

"Why?"

"Because he is afraid of being kidnaped," Miss Ruysdale said. "He is also afraid of being poisoned. He is also afraid of accidental death. Do you know why he hasn't been back to this country for seventeen years? Because he's afraid to fly and he's afraid to travel on any public carrier, including an ocean liner."

"How is he coming?" I asked.

Miss Ruysdale gave me her Mona Lisa smile. "In two ocean-going yachts," she said.

"Two?"

"He owns them both. He travels in one and the other follows in case something happens to the first one."

"You're kidding!"

"He has two private chefs. One cooks his meals and the other — "

" — is there in case something happens to the first one? Right?"

"Right. He has his personal doctor within calling distance day and night. His man, Allerton, tastes all his food before he eats anything. He has two personal armed bodyguards, one for the daytime and one for the nights." Miss Ruysdale's smile widened. "And he has two secretaries, one for the daytime — "

" — and one for the nights. Which one is Shelda?"

"Whenever he has a thought worth preserving, he needs someone there to take it down — day or night."

"And the boss has turned over his penthouse because — "

"Because he has sympathy for anyone who lives in such mortal terror."

In the elevator I glanced at the figure hidden from me by the mink collar and the hat brim. I understood the two Cadillacs. The second one was in case something happened to the first one. I wondered what the night secretary really did. Shelda was still looking at the toe of her shoe.

★ ★ ★

Chambrun was standing with his back to the fireplace in the large living room of the penthouse, smoking one of his flat-shaped Egyptian cigarettes. He watched the procession come in, his eyes hooded. He watched Ed Butler, the bodyguard, move swiftly through the living room into the rest of the apartment. Evidently he was making sure that no one was hidden under a bed.

Battle stood in the middle of the room, still shrouded in mink and felt. He didn't speak. Dr. Cobb was struggling with an asthmatic cough. Allerton, his bowler removed, stood at attention, waiting for something. None of the Battle party spoke except Shelda.

"Hello, Mr. Chambrun," she said.

"Nice to see you back here, Shelda," he said. He looked at me and I saw that his eyes were amused.

The bodyguard reappeared. "All clear, Mr. Battle," he said.

Allerton sprang into action. He turned down the mink collar and he took the hat. I don't know what I'd expected, but what I saw was the wreckage of what must have been an extraordinarily beautiful young man. The face was like a lovely piece of china, cracked and stained. The eyes were blue and very bright, the cheekbones prominent, the delicate mouth drooped a little as though George Battle was about to burst into tears.

"Hello, Pierre," he said. The voice was soft, almost musical.

"Welcome," Chambrun said. "I see you made it safely."

"I'm exhausted from the tension of it," Battle said. "Has Gaston arrived?"

"He's in the kitchen," Chambrun said. "I believe he has prepared some hot bouillon and dry crackers for you — knowing your taste on such occasions."

"Thank God," Battle said. He tottered toward an armchair. "Allerton!"

"At once, Mr. George," Allerton said, and headed toward the kitchen.

"It's generous of you, Pierre, to turn over your place to me," Battle said. "It seems so much easier to protect than rooms in the main body of the hotel."

"I understand," Chambrun said. He glanced at the bodyguard. "My security man, Jerry Dodd, will be here presently to discuss round-the-clock arrangements with you."

"You trust this Dodd?" Butler asked.

"With my life," Chambrun said.

"What I'm concerned with is Mr. Battle's life," Butler said.

"Bully for you," Chambrun said, the amusement faded from his eyes. "Is there anything I can do for you, George?"

"I understand the film people have arrived."

Chambrun glanced at me and I nodded.

"Please get word to Mr. Maxwell that I — "

"Mr. Maxwell Zorn," Allerton said in a stage whisper.

" — get word to Mr. Zorn that I can't possibly see anyone tonight; that I'm exhausted and will be till tomorrow morning. However, if they want to see Miss Mason — " So many words seemed to have done him in. He lowered what looked like paper-thin eyelids.

Shelda, who looked as though she hadn't heard, appeared to be studying a beautiful Matisse that hung on the far wall. Why, I wondered, would Maxie Zorn want to see her? Then I felt a cold finger run down my spine. Was she in line for that seven minutes of public lovemaking with David Loring in the epic? I told myself I would damn well put a stop to that, and realized at once that if Shelda wanted to, Shelda would.

"If you have any problems about security, George, the switchboard operator can reach me wherever I am," Chambrun said. "Mark and I will leave you to rest." He gave me a sign that he was ready to leave.

I tried to will Shelda to look at me, but it didn't work.

In the elevator Chambrun gave me a wry smile. "A year wasn't enough," he said.

"Meaning?"

"Shelda," he said. "Lovely girl."

"Is she thinking of becoming a movie actress?"

Chambrun took his silver cigarette case from his pocket and tapped a cigarette on the back of it. "It would please George Battle," he said.

"To hell with George Battle!"

"Don't be possessive," Chambrun said. "You retired a year ago, remember?"

Oh, I had retired, in a kind of small boy pique a year ago. Shelda and I had been living together for two years, very much in love, very happy. She'd had an apartment about a block and a half from the Beaumont. I kept clothes there, and shaving things, and my private life. Shelda was early women's lib. I was vintage puritan in a way. I wanted to marry her. Every day that we spent together I wanted her more, and was more afraid of losing her. I suppose I saw marriage as a trap she couldn't escape. I guess she saw it the same way. It got to be an almost daily debate and some of the joy went out of being together. Chambrun needed someone to go to France with special papers for George Battle to sign, and he offered Shelda the chance to be his messenger. The shrewd little bastard sensed that we needed to be separated for a spell. It looked like a couple of weeks. So Shelda went and when she got there, she wrote me a 'dear John' letter. It was clear that unless she gave in to me we just couldn't go on together. She needed much more time than two weeks to come to a decision. Mr. Battle had offered her a permanent job and she was going to take it. I had nightmares in which Mr. Battle was some kind of Casanova and all the dark, handsome Frenchmen in the world were waiting in line for her. She didn't answer letters. I had blown it, and very slowly I began to learn to live with that as a fact. Now, in the space of twenty-five minutes, I was hooked again.

"I suggest you convey George's message to Maxie Zorn," Chambrun said. "You may be able to find out whether your lady is really a candidate for the big sex scene with the Golden Boy. Talk to Peter Potter."

"Who is Peter Potter?"

"Public relations man for Zorn. If you saw them arrive, you must have seen him. He's a dwarf."

"That one!"

"A very witty, very bitter, very charming little man," Chambrun said. "If he chooses, he can tell you the truth, which may be more complex than you imagine." The elevator stopped at the second floor where Chambrun gave me a gentle pat on the shoulder and went along to his office. I continued down to the lobby.

★ ★ ★

The Beaumont's lobby normally has a kind of cathedral quiet and elegance. It had been thrown completely out of

24

character by the arrival of David Loring. The Golden Boy had disappeared along with his entourage when I got there, but the memory lingered on. The place was still crowded with gabbling, breathless women. I had the feeling they might camp out there until the glamour boy took off for some other sanctuary. The Spartan Bar, normally reserved for elderly gentlemen who played marathon games of chess, had been invaded by females. A glance upward told me that the Trapeze Bar on the mezzanine was bursting at the seams.

"What we need is a bull horn," Johnny Thacker, the bell captain, said at my elbow. "David-baby isn't going to show again tonight. Dinner party arranged for in Fourteen-B, his suite. Did you get a look at that dame he had with him?"

"Briefly."

"Angela Adams, said to be our David's number-one candidate for private and public lovemaking. Raquel Welch is an also-ran beside Angela-baby."

"Where is Zorn located?" I asked. I hoped Johnny was right. If Angela Adams was David Loring's choice for the epic, then Shelda was almost certainly out. Loring would surely have his way.

"Maxie-baby is in 1421, right next to Golden Boy and Golden Girl," Johnny said. "Excuse. Some nut is drawing phallic symbols on the wall over there."

The Beaumont was having it tough. If Chambrun knew what was happening, he'd probably appear, point imperiously to the front door, and the ladies would all slink away with their tails between their legs. He had that kind of command.

I found Maxie Zorn alone in 1421. He was dark, slim, with a long nose and black eyes that seemed to burn. He was highly irritated by the message I delivered.

"Crazy bastard!" he said. "He's exhausted from crossing a very calm ocean in a luxury yacht that makes

Onassis look like a pauper. He's got to rest while hundreds of people are waiting for the word."

"What word?"

He looked at me as if I was some kind of idiot child. "Money, friend. Haven't you ever heard of money? Mr. George Battle is the money behind my film, or will be when he says yes. You know this Mason doll?"

"Yes, I know the Mason doll," I said, feeling my jaw muscles tighten. "She used to be my secretary."

"Maybe I can use you," Maxie said.

"I wouldn't try," I said.

The black eyes burned into me. "Can you imagine why she hesitates?" he asked.

"I don't know what you're talking about," I said.

"You've read about the big moment in this picture of mine?"

"Who hasn't?"

"We're offering your Miss Mason the part," he said, "and she can't make up her mind. Would you believe there's seven million bucks on the line?"

"Probably not."

"That's what Battle has agreed to put up to finance my film — under two conditions. Condition number one, the Mason doll is to play the big scene in the raw with David. Condition number two, he is to have five prints of the film. Of course a share of the profits, chum, and there will be profits. And the Mason dame can't make up her mind! How do you like that for dizzy blonde thinking?"

"Probably not everyone thinks that rolling around with David Loring is the key to happiness," I said.

"The hell with that. We're offering her a hundred and fifty thousand dollars for seven minutes' exposure on film and she can't make up her mind. Talk to her for me. Don't tell her I said so, but I'll go to a quarter of a million if she's trying to make a tough deal with me. It's worth a quarter of a million to get seven."

"Why does Battle want five prints of

the film?" I heard myself ask.

"To warm up his old age, I suspect," Zorn said. "He'll probably keep looking at those seven minutes until he's worn out all five prints."

"You mean he's a dirty old man?"

"I mean he's a screw pot."

"There must be plenty of beautiful girls who'd jump at the chance," I said.

"Battle wants her and nobody else," Zorn said. "So it doesn't matter if she's wall-eyed and knock-kneed. We'll make that popular if we have to. Will you talk to her?"

"I promise," I said. My ten cents' worth was not going to help him.

But I didn't get the chance that evening. My spies informed me that Shelda was one of the dinner guests in David Loring's suite. He was evidently using his personal charms to persuade her.

★ ★ ★

My normal routine in the evening is to climb into a dinner jacket about seven o'clock and circulate. Shelda used to say I was like Marshal Dillon putting Dodge City to bed for the night. There was always someone to talk to, some celebrity staying with us for a spell, someone to drink with. My job was to promote people who wanted a little promotion and to keep others under cover. Then there were fashion designers and buyers who use the hotel often for special showings, society people planning charity functions, people concerned with special social or diplomatic banquets. And just lonely people who like to talk.

That night I didn't want to talk. This cockamaney business about Shelda and the Maxie Zorn film had me climbing the walls. I could imagine her up there in 14-B with Golden Boy, being sold a bill of goods. They might even be practicing!

I'm a slow drinker and I hold my liquor pretty well. I have to in my job.

That night I was pouring it on at a pretty good clip. About ten o'clock I was in the Trapeze Bar with Eddie, the head bartender, giving me the fish eye when Mr. Del Greco, the captain, touched me on the shoulder and told me I was wanted on the phone. It was Mrs. Kiley, the chief night operator on the switchboard.

"Mr. Haskell?"

"Probably," I said.

"You're wanted on the double in the boss's penthouse," she told me. She sounded uptight.

"What's wrong?" I asked her.

"Somebody just tried to kill Mr. Battle," she said.

2

ON the way up in the elevator I didn't take it too seriously. By that time I was thinking of George Battle as a degenerate old creep, scared of his own shadow. Somebody had probably said "Boo!" to him unexpectedly. That could bring on a breakdown, I told myself.

But when I stepped off the elevator at the penthouse level, I saw that it wasn't a joke. One of Jerry Dodd's men, Art Stein, was standing outside the front door. He was fish-belly pale.

"How the hell he ever got in is beyond me," Art said. "Three of us patrolling the outside, never in one place for a minute."

"Who got in where?" I asked.

"Some jerk wearing a stocking mask. Took a shot at Mr. Battle in his bed. Then, somehow he got away, which is just as impossible as getting in."

"Is Battle hurt?"

"The bullet missed him by about six inches," Art said, "but the old boy may have had a heart attack, Jerry says."

Art gave the doorbell some kind of a signal ring and it was promptly opened by Ed Butler, Battle's guntoter. Butler looked nasty. Before I could say anything, he began to slap over my clothes, evidently looking for concealed weapons. He wasn't gentle and I protested.

"You hold still if you don't want your effing neck broken," he said. Finally he was satisfied that I wasn't carrying a hand grenade and let me in.

Chambrun and Jerry Dodd were alone in the living room. Jerry Dodd, our security officer, is short, thin, wiry tough with ice-cold blue eyes. He predates me at the Beaumont, and I guess that next to Miss Ruysdale he comes as close to being indispensable as anyone on Chambrun's staff.

"Hell to pay," Chambrun said, and his eyes were those of the hanging judge at that moment. Anyone who disturbs the efficient routines of the Beaumont, anyone who commits a violence or a nuisance on the premises, has made himself a mortal enemy.

"What happened?" I asked.

"Old man went to bed about nine o'clock," Jerry said in his crisp, cool voice. "I had three men acting as sentries on the roof. Seemed kind of nonsensical, but they were there, goddamn'. Inside was Butler, sitting outside the bedroom door reading a magazine. Allerton and the chef, Gaston, and Dr. Cobb were in their respective rooms. They all heard the gunshot, so did my men outside. Butler was the first one in the room. Mr. Battle was sitting up in bed, light on at the bedside table, covers pulled up around him, screaming. Bedroom window on the north side was open. As you know, it's barred, because it's flush with the side of the building — twenty-four floor drop, for Christ sake. Butler ran into the bathroom, which also opens into the hall. No one in sight. By then Allerton and the chef were there. No one had seen or heard anything but the gunshot. They finally got some kind of sense out of Battle. He'd been asleep. He woke up, suddenly certain that there was someone in the room. He reached out and turned on the bedside lamp. What he says he saw was a man wearing a stocking mask with a gun aimed at the bed. The instant the light came on the man fired. Bullet's buried in the headboard about six inches from Battle's forehead. According to Battle, the man cried out — something unintelligible — and ran into the bathroom. No one else saw him or heard him. Disappeared into thin air."

"It's just possible," Chambrun said, scowling. "Butler breaks into the room, the gunman runs out through the bathroom, doubles back past the door through which Butler has gone, and makes it out to the vestibule."

"The minute the shot was fired my man on the roof nearest the door stepped into the vestibule," Jerry said. "Twenty seconds, maybe. He looked at the elevator indicator and saw that the car was down in the lobby."

"Fire stairs," Chambrun said.

"Bolted on the inside," Jerry said. "You can't leave by the fire door and lock it behind you."

"He got across the roof to the next penthouse," I said.

"Only just possible. My two men outside were standing by, guns drawn. I say 'possible' only because there isn't any other way."

"Your men weren't doing what they were supposed to be doing," I said.

Jerry gave me a bitter little smile. "I'll be denying that to the cops and the District Attorney for the next month. I know those guys."

The door to the bedroom opened and Dr. Cobb came out. The fat man was wearing a food-stained dressing gown. He found a cigarette in a torn pocket and lit it with unsteady hands.

"He wants you in there, Edward, sitting beside his bed," Cobb said to the bodyguard. "You better hold his hand nicely, Edward. You don't smell like roses to him right now."

Butler went into the bedroom, muttering something about this being an effing injustice world. Dr. Cobb's watery eyes were roving anxiously around the room. I knew the look of an alcoholic desperate for a drink.

"Liquor in that Chinese cabinet, Doctor," Chambrun said.

"God bless you," Cobb said. He opened the cabinet and poured himself five fingers of Jack Daniels in a highball glass. He tossed it down like water. "Lifesaver," he said.

"The patient?" Chambrun asked.

"He's never as sick as he appears to be," Cobb said. "But he had the bewadding scared out of him, Mr. Chambrun. That bullet missed him by inches. I've given him a sedative. He'll sleep presently, scared or not." He took a deep, wheezing breath. "Puzzling thing. The man wanted to kill him, yet when the light came on and he had a clear shot at him, he only fired once, missing."

"Maybe he thought he'd frighten him to death," I said.

Jerry Dodd gave me an odd look. "Maybe when the light went on he saw he had the wrong man," he said.

Chambrun's heavy lids lifted.

"Not very many people knew that you wouldn't be sleeping in your bed tonight, boss," Jerry said. "When he saw it wasn't you, he managed to jerk off that first shot a little wild and went away. How does it go? 'Come again another day'?"

Dr. Cobb reached for the Jack Daniels bottle.

★ ★ ★

One thing you don't do with Chambrun in a serious situation that involves the hotel is make jokes. I was a little tight, angry over Battle's desire to have Shelda make a sex movie, and thinking everything was pretty comic about this two-yacht, two-chef, two-Cadillac tycoon. I'd been prepared to believe this whole thing was some kind of psychotic charade — until Jerry said what he did. Jerry was making a serious suggestion.

Chambrun didn't comment. His eyes were hidden again, deep in their pouches.

Jerry didn't let go of his idea. "Any minute now we're going to be swarmed under by cops," he said. "Homicide cops, assistant D.A.'s, maybe the D.A. himself. Mr. George Battle is the richest man in the world."

"The second richest," Dr. Cobb wheezed. He'd poured himself a second massive slug of bourbon.

"Newspapers, the media," Jerry said. "Everybody's going to be digging into the Battle history: how he got so rich, how much of the world he controls, the hotel in detail, his love life, his health, who hates him, who could have a motive for trying to kill him. And all the while some character is hanging around the fringes waiting to take a second shot at you, boss."

Chambrun's smile was wry. "So how did I get so rich, how much of the world do I control, what about my love life, my health, and who hates me."

"I'm not laughing," Jerry said. "Let me say that it's a miracle this guy got in here and got out again. There's only one realistic way it could have been done."

"The fire stairs," Chambrun said.

"Right. Someone who knows the hotel in detail. Someone who came up here earlier in the day and threw the bolt on the fire stairs door. I didn't check it personally when I came up here. I'm afraid I took it for granted. It was a way into the vestibule that we may have overlooked."

"And how did he get through the front door?"

"Someone connected with the staff, planning long in advance, could have gotten a duplicate key made. From the housekeeper's set."

"And how did he get past Butler, sitting outside the bedroom door with a gun in his lap?" Chambrun asked.

"Human fallibility," Jerry said. "Butler will deny it with his dying breath, but he could have fallen asleep."

"Wouldn't this killer of yours have been surprised to find a bodyguard outside my door, if he knows so much about the hotel and me?"

"It's a good question," Jerry admitted.

"And the three men on the roof?"

"If he came by the fire stairs, he'd have no reason to know they were there. Look, boss. Take it seriously. The guy is after you. He's planned a way to get in. He finds a guy sitting outside your bedroom door, asleep, a gun in his lap. He's puzzled, but he's in. He decides not to blow it. He tiptoes down the hall, into the bathroom, through it to the bedroom.

He knows the layout. He knows where your bed is located in the room. He's going to pour lead into where the pillow ought to be. Then the light goes on. His finger is on the trigger and he squeezes. But a fraction of a second of light shows him it's not you in the bed. The shot misses. He cries out in surprise and splits. But there's a silver lining to every cloud. Nobody's going to be looking for him. They're going to be looking for someone who might want to rub out George Battle. So he waits for another good moment. You don't take it seriously, boss, and you're a walking dead man."

"What do you want me to do?" Chambrun asked. "Lock myself in my office until you pin the tail on this donkey?"

"If I didn't know better, I'd say yes to that," Jerry said. "I want to cover you every minute, day and night. If there's an intelligent cop on the case, I want to alert him to the fact he's looking for the wrong guy. Let Mark and Betsy Ruysdale run your routine errands for you so I can keep you covered. I want to check out on every guest in the hotel and recheck the entire staff, along with a list of people that may have been fired in the last year." Jerry ran slender fingers through his sleek, dark hair. "I want to keep you safe, boss."

"Thanks for being concerned, Jerry," Chambrun said, "but if I have to walk around my own hotel scared, I might just as well be dead. What am I supposed to do, say 'please, sir, may I go to the bathroom'?"

"Stubborn bastard!" Jerry said.

Chambrun smiled. "At least that makes you sound less like a mother hen."

The doorbell rang, and a moment later we were inundated by cops, police photographers, a young man from the D.A.'s office. In the confusion Jerry had me by the arm.

"Get hold of Betsy Ruysdale," he said. "She'd be intuitive about anyone who might want to get the boss."

"You believe that's the way it is?" I asked.

"I'm not going to risk its being any other way," he said.

For a few moments the elements of a mad comedy stayed with us. Dr. Cobb, his stained dressing gown drawn around him like a toga, was blocking the way into the bedroom.

"You can't go in there," he told two young plainclothes cops who were trying to push him aside. His cigarette bobbed up and down between his flabby lips.

"That's where it's at!" one of the cops shouted at him.

"The man in there is my patient," Dr. Cobb said. "It would be dangerous to his survival for you all to go barging in there. I must forbid it."

"Out of the way, dad," one of the cops said.

"I think you better think about it," Chambrun said. There was authority in his voice that made the two plainclothes men turn his way. "I'm Pierre Chambrun, the hotel manager. The doctor is right. Mr. Battle is suffering from shock. He might not survive any more excitement."

"You might be guilty of murder," Dr. Cobb said. He couldn't say any more because he appeared to be choking to death on cigarette smoke.

At that point Allerton, wearing a neat, white houseman's coat, appeared in the door from the kitchen. "Would anyone care for coffee?" he asked.

I draw the curtain there.

★ ★ ★

There is only one elevator that goes all the way up to the penthouse level. The rest stop at the twenty-fourth floor. Jerry Dodd had commandeered the penthouse car so that no one not wanted at the top could get there. The main stairway and the fire stairs were blocked off by Jerry's men.

I had sobered up rather abruptly and

I wasn't laughing any more. Jerry's theory that Chambrun was the real target had helped the sobering process. Jerry and Chambrun would probably be embroiled with cops and the D.A.'s man for the next hour or so and I figured I could get things rolling. I could locate Miss Ruysdale and start checking out on the list of guests to see if there were any suggestive names on it.

I went down the stairway to the twenty-fourth floor and was let out by Jerry's men. That's as far as I got for a while. The corridor I walked into was jammed with people. I recognized several newspapermen who'd, somehow, gotten the word. There were rubberneckers, and some employees, and a little way off I saw Maxie Zorn, Peter Potter, the four-foot Mephisto, and Shelda.

I had a time fighting my way to them. The reporters were all over me. I tried 'no comment' for a while, but I saw I wasn't going to get out of there alive with that, so I held up my hand for silence and, miraculously, got it.

"I'm not authorized to make any kind of statement," I said. "But I can tell you that someone took a shot at George Battle and missed. Battle isn't physically hurt, but he's in shock."

"Who was it?"

"Have they got him?"

"The cops have only just arrived," I told them.

"You don't know who it was, Mark? He got away?"

"So help me, no answers yet," I said.

By then Maxie Zorn had me by the coat lapels. "I've got to get to him, Haskell," he said. "If he's in any kind of danger, we've got to settle our deal."

Potter, the dwarf, looked up at me, his brown eyes dancing. "Your money or your life — in that order," he said. "Someone really shot at him?"

"Really. Missed by about six inches," I said.

"I'd have bet my best silk shirt he wouldn't have survived that."

"He may not," I said.

"Oh, God, I've got to get to him," Zorn said. "Can't you explain to those creeps on the door that I have to get to him?"

"Every man is said to have his price," I said. "You could try."

"I think I could be helpful to him," Shelda said.

I let myself look at her for the first time. "How were Golden Boy's etchings?" I asked her.

"Oh, Mark, you idiot!"

"Sorry, friends, I have work to do," I said.

There was no trouble getting to the down-elevator. Everyone and his brother was trying to come up. As I stepped into the car, I realized that Shelda was with me.

"There's no point in pretending we're strangers, Mark," she said.

"Who's pretending?" I said. I felt butterflies in my stomach. I knew I didn't care who'd been shot at or who was in danger. I wanted her so badly it hurt.

The car started its noiseless descent. I had pressed the second-floor button. Chambrun's office and my apartment were both located on two. Shelda stood across the car from me. She was wearing a pale blue dinner dress of some kind of shiny material that seemed to fit her lovely figure like a glove. She was carrying a silver evening bag and there was a gardenia pinned to her shoulder which, I told myself bitterly, must have been put there by Golden Boy. I wasn't making much sense, you understand, with an attempted murder upstairs and Chambrun in danger. I wanted to hurt her.

"Did you have to strip down so David-baby could see whether you meet his specifications?" I asked.

"There doesn't seem to be much point in trying to talk to you," she said, her eyes averted.

"What did you want to talk about?"

"Among other things I'd wanted to tell you how very glad I am to see you, Mark. Evidently that doesn't matter to you."

Of course it mattered like hell, but I was still involved in playing the jealous adolescent. "It's a great opportunity for any girl," I said, "the chance to roll around in the hay with David-baby."

"I haven't said yes," she said, still not looking at me.

"I have news for you. Zorn will raise the price to a quarter of a million if you play hard to get."

"There doesn't seem to be much point in trying to talk to you about it," she said. "Please, tell me what happened upstairs."

I told her, winding up with Jerry's fear that the attack had really been meant for Chambrun. She listened, frowning that intense little frown that always reminded me of a small child puzzling over an arithmetic problem about apples and oranges.

The car had stopped at the second

floor and the doors opened.

"I think maybe I should talk to you and Mr. Chambrun," Shelda said, "no matter how distasteful that may be for you." She walked out of the car and down the corridor toward Chambrun's office.

My intention had been to look up Miss Ruysdale's private, unlisted home phone number, so that she could be gotten to work on our guest list as Jerry had suggested. I should have known better. Miss Ruysdale was at her desk in the outer office when Shelda and I walked in. I'll never know whether she has some secret organization that alerts her to everything, or whether she is just plain psychic when it comes to Chambrun and his needs. Ruysdale is on the tall side, with dark red hair, thick, cut short and worn like a duck-tailed cap. She has a straight nose, a high forehead and cheekbones, and a wide mouth. She is almost classically beautiful. She is, I know, all woman but she affects an almost

51

male severity in her dress and manner. Chambrun would want his secretary to be attractive, but not some doll who would have all the male staff salivating over her. I suspect Ruysdale may be the most interesting woman I know, but I've never been able to penetrate beyond her efficient, friendly-but-impersonal office manner.

"Hello, you two," she said.

Shelda gave her a quick girl-embrace.

"Jerry wants you to — " I began.

"I have the registration cards here," Ruysdale said. "I've started to go through them."

Guests at the Beaumont might not be pleased to know how much we really know about them. There is a special card for each guest and there is a code used which tells more than the guest might like. The code letter A means the subject is an alcoholic; W on a man's card means he is a woman chaser, possibly a customer for the expensive call girls who sometimes are seen in the Trapeze Bar; M on a woman's card means she's a manhunter; O means the guest is 'over his head', can't afford the Beaumont's prices and shouldn't be allowed to get in too deep; MX on a married man's card means he's double-crossing his wife, and WX means the wife is cuckolding the husband. The small letter 'd' means diplomatic connections. If there is special information about the guest, it is attached in memo form to the card, and if that information is not meant to be public knowledge in the front office, the card is marked with Chambrun's initials, meaning that the boss has special knowledge about the guest in his private file.

Ruysdale was holding out a card to me.

"You're a wonder," I said as I took the card. "How did you know?"

"No miracle," she said. "Karl Nevers phoned me that there was trouble in the penthouse." Nevers is the night manager on the front desk. "First thing that occurred to me is that it might have been meant for Mr. Chambrun."

I glanced at the card. "Richard Cleaves," I read out loud. "Room 1419. He must be part of Zorn's group."

"He wrote the novel that Zorn's film is based on," Shelda said. "*A Man's World.* Have either of you read it? It's really a very good novel."

"Especially the nude scenes," I said. I looked at the card again when I saw Shelda blush. Chambrun's initials were lettered in the corner. "What's the scoop on him?" I asked.

"Only Mr. Chambrun and God know what's in the private file," Ruysdale said. She was thumbing through more cards.

"Is Cleaves blond, crew cut, black glasses?" I asked.

Shelda nodded. I remembered him coming in at the rear of David Loring's cavalcade. "And there are no nude scenes in the novel," Shelda said, unexpectedly sharp. "They've been added for the film."

I put the card down on Ruysdale's

desk. "I wonder what's so special about Master Cleaves," I said.

"He's a very interesting but a very cold and distant young man," Shelda said. "He came to see Mr. Battle in France when discussion of the film came up."

"Cold and distant isn't your type," I said.

Miss Ruysdale gave me a bored look. "Why don't you grow up, Mark?" she said. "If you're concerned about Mr. Chambrun, why not get to work on some of these cards."

She was right, of course. I was behaving badly.

"The reason I came with you, Mark," Shelda said, "was that I thought Mr. Chambrun ought to know about Richard Cleaves."

"He evidently does know something," Ruysdale said, fingering the card with Chambrun's initials on it.

"It was about three months ago," Shelda said. "Maxie Zorn made an appointment to see Mr. Battle at his villa in Cannes. I didn't make the appointment. Gloria, his daytime secretary, made it."

"Before you go any further," I said, "would you mind telling me what the duties of the nighttime secretary are?"

"Do shut up, Mark," Ruysdale said.

Shelda gave me a steady look. "Mr. Battle rarely sleeps more than an hour at a time," she said. "He catnaps day and night. When he's awake, his mind is never not working. He has thoughts about business, about a memoire he's writing, about world affairs. The moment he has an idea, he rings for his secretary, whichever one is on duty, and dictates. Sometimes it is only a sentence or two. Sometimes he'll go on for a couple of hours. We have a stenotype machine — the kind a court stenographer uses — so he can go on as long as he wants."

"And you pop out of bed whenever he has an idea?"

"I sleep in the daytime," Shelda

said. "May I tell you about Richard Cleaves?"

"If he opens his mouth again, I'll send him to his room with bread and water," Ruysdale said.

"Gloria made the appointment and it was in his book when I took over that day. It just said 'Maxwell Zorn'. But three of them came: Zorn, Peter Potter, and Cleaves. I had to get clearance from Mr. Battle before Cleaves and Potter could be let through the front gate. He seemed not to know who Potter and Cleaves were, but he allowed them to come in. Naturally I was surprised when I saw Potter. He's a dwarf, you know, but a nice little man, very witty, fun to talk with. Cleaves was the way he always is, handsome but cold, distant, his expression hidden by those black glasses. I don't recap Gloria's notes, so I had no idea why they were there, but I knew Maxwell Zorn was in the film business and that Cleaves had written a best-selling novel. Potter seemed like a sort of court jester. I wasn't asked to sit in on their conference. As soon as they were gone, Mr. Battle sent for me.

"'I have agreed, under certain conditions, to finance a film for Maxwell Zorn', he said. 'Make a note of the date and the time. And I want an airmail-special delivery letter sent to Pierre Chambrun in New York'. Then he gave me the letter. I remember it quite clearly. 'Pierre: Richard Cleaves, author of A Man's World, is in reality Richard St. Germaine. You should be warned that he hasn't forgotten'. It was marked 'Personal' and mailed that afternoon."

"Forgotten what?" I asked.

"You don't ask Mr. Battle that kind of question," Shelda said. "I never saw any of them again until just before we left France. Then Peter turned up at the villa."

"Peter?"

"Peter Potter."

"So you're on first-name terms with him?"

"Careful, Mark," Ruysdale said.

"He came to see me," Shelda said. A faint spot of color appeared in her cheeks. "That was the first time that I heard that Mr. Battle wanted me to — to act in the film. That I was one of the conditions he'd made for putting up the money for the film. Mr. Battle had never mentioned it to me."

"That is rather odd, don't you think?" Ruysdale said. It kept me from some other inanity.

"Not if you know Mr. Battle," Shelda said. "Peter came to offer me the part. He said Mr. Zorn and Richard Cleaves had seen me and both felt, at once, that I was the girl they wanted for it. I said no. Then Peter mentioned a sum of money — a very large sum of money. I was startled, but I still said no. Then he told me the truth. It was Mr. Battle who wanted me to take it. It was one of his conditions. 'I think he meant to do you a favor', Peter said. 'If you tell him you don't want it, he may drop it as a condition'. He gave me his charming smile. 'It's very important to us'."

"Seven million dollars' worth," I said.

"I went to Mr. Battle," Shelda said. "He was very sweet about it. He told me he had made my getting the part a condition. He hadn't told me because he'd wanted me to think that Mr. Zorn and the others had chosen me. He saw it as an opportunity for me to make a great deal of money and possibly develop a glamorous career. He had meant it as a gesture of gratitude to me for the year of work I'd given him. He advised me to — to overcome my reluctance to appear in the nude. The Victorian age was long gone, he said. He urged me not to give a final answer until I'd had a chance to think about it, perhaps talk about it with someone close."

"Like maybe David-baby?" I said.

Shelda looked straight at me for the first time. "He suggested you, Mark — someone who'd once been in love with me and would have my best interests at heart."

"So ask me what I think!" I said.

"I don't think I could trust you to be disinterested," she said.

"I don't think I can trust either of you to remember we've got a would-be assassin running around the hotel and that Mr. Chambrun may be the target," Ruysdale said.

"What about this Richard Cleaves who 'hasn't forgotten', Shelda?"

"Have you been prying into my private files, Ruysdale?" Chambrun's voice was cold and so unexpected that we all spun around like guilty children.

He was standing in the office door, his eyes narrowed slits, his hands jammed into the pockets of his jacket.

"I — I'm to blame, Mr. Chambrun," Shelda said. "I took Mr. Battle's dictation — a note to you. When I heard you were in danger, I remembered and I — I told Mark and Miss Ruysdale."

Chambrun drew a deep breath. "What Richard Cleaves hasn't forgotten," he said, "is that I gave the order to have his father executed, and that George Battle paid for the rope that hanged him."

He walked past us and into his office.

3

THERE had been a time in Chambrun's life, when he was a very young man, perhaps thirty years ago, which he referred to infrequently as 'the dark days'. Born a Frenchman, his parents had brought him to this country when he was a small child. He had started out working as a busboy in some small restaurant on New York's East Side run by a distant relative. He had decided that the restaurant or hotel business was to be his future and he had studied management under the relative and eventually gone to Cornell for special training. While he was there, the war had broken out in Europe and France had been overrun by the Nazis. Chambrun was now an American citizen, but some kind of intense fury at what was happening to his French brothers took hold of him. He has never told me how he got back to Europe, but he managed, and made contact with the Resistance. I gather that at age twenty-one or-two he became an inspirational leader in the underground fight against the German conquerors. I know this not from him but from a half dozen French diplomats who have stayed at the Beaumont and who speak of Pierre Chambrun as a kind of legendary hero.

I knew, as he left us, from the way he spoke, that he was referring to 'the dark days."

Chambrun's office is not like an office at all, except for the three telephones on his carved Florentine desk. It is large and airy. The magnificent oriental rug on the floor had been a gift from a Far Eastern prince whom Chambrun had saved at some time from a predatory lady. Facing his desk is a Picasso, the blue period, personally inscribed by the artist. The furniture is substantial, comfortable.

On a teakwood sideboard is a Turkish coffeemaker that is constantly in operation. After two cups of Colombian coffee for breakfast Chambrun drinks that foul Turkish brew the rest of the day and night. There is a portable bar with every liquor and liqueur on it you can imagine. Chambrun drinks very little himself, mostly wine from the Beaumont's unexcelled cellar, but he is a ready host.

Ruysdale is rarely uncertain about Chambrun's moods, but on this occasion she seemed doubtful whether or not to follow him. She picked up the Cleaves card from her desk, frowned at it, and then made up her mind. She walked briskly into the office, and Shelda and I followed her.

Chambrun was seated at his desk, his eyes squinted against the smoke from his cigarette. He was silent for moments, lost in some kind of private reverie, and then he looked at us.

"Would it shock you to know that Claude St. Germaine was not the only man I had hanged in the dark days?" he asked.

None of us spoke.

"It was just thirty years ago," he said. "The boy couldn't have been more than four or five years old."

"The boy?" Ruysdale asked in her flat, businesslike voice.

"Richard. Richard St. Germaine," Chambrun said. He seemed to sink deeper into his chair. "We live with violence and terrorism all around us today. The Arab-Israeli thing; the Olympic games last year, the letter bombs; the Mafia killings in our own streets. We cry out against it; it's evil, vicious, uncivilized. And yet — " he took a deep drag on his cigarette and let the smoke out in a long, curling stream — "and yet thirty years ago, in the dark days, we practiced it and we thought it righteous and heroic. I saw Claude St. Germaine hanging from a lamppost outside the Nazi military headquarters in Paris and I felt good about it." The corner of Chambrun's mouth twitched.

"I had given the orders for it, I helped with the actual deed, and, God help me, I felt good about it."

"What had he done?" Shelda asked. It was almost a whisper.

Chambrun looked at her. "There were two kinds of enemy in those days," he said. "There were the German soldiers and the Nazi SS men; and there were the collaborators, Frenchmen who helped the Germans turn our whole country into a prison camp. We hated the German soldiers and SS men, but they were men under orders; they wore uniforms we could recognize, they were armed and ready to kill us, and we fought each other, fighting, hiding, sniping, hiding again. Somehow it was a decent fight, even though they were animals!" He crushed out his cigarette in the copper ash tray on his desk and took a fresh one from his case and lit it. I thought his voice shook a little as he went on. "But the collaborators! They were civilians like us, Frenchmen like us, and yet they served the enemy, eagerly, willingly. They betrayed their countrymen; they allowed their homes, their money, their prewar friendships, to be used against their own people. Claude St. Germaine was one of them. He gave magnificent parties for them in his great house on the Avenue Kleber. He sat in their councils. Publicly he appeared to be a Frenchman grieving for his motherland; he even approached us and gave us bits of information which would presumably help us. The big parties, he told us, were given against his will. He was helpless. Following tips we got from him, we countered one or two minor Nazi plots. We came to trust him. And then he let us on to a big event. Hitler himself was to visit the house on the Avenue Kleber. St. Germaine showed us how we could get into the house through the sewers and old wine cellars under the house. He drew maps for us. He provided us with duplicated keys. Twenty of our best men went to the house the night Hitler was supposed to be there. I would have been there myself except for the mischance of a badly sprained ankle which limited my mobility. Our twenty saboteurs would destroy the house and assassinate Hitler and his top people — except that it was a trap, carefully set up by the Nazis with the aid of St. Germaine. All twenty men were caught in a center room and slaughtered. They were most of our key men, our best men, and St. Germaine had contrived to eliminate them and almost break the backbone of our movement, of the Resistance itself. That was how I, at twenty-two, became one of the leaders. Our top men had all been killed in ten minutes of bloody horror." Chambrun was silent for a moment, and then he went on. "The first order I gave was that St. Germaine should be hanged like a common murderer — which is what he was — and his body displayed so that all collaborators should know what was in store for them. It took a month to trap him. It took five minutes to try him in a kangaroo court. It took another five minutes to hang him by the neck until he was dead. It took a diversionary action to distract attention from the front of the Avenue Kleber house, and while the Germans and the collaborating police were chasing us down back alleys three of us hung St. Germaine's body on a lamppost at the front for all the world to see. It seemed, as I said, just and fair and even heroic. Man's morality depends on where he sits, on his perspective, on his personal emotions. We saw what we had done as right and proper. Richard Cleaves sees us as villains."

"But he was only five years old, you said," Ruysdale said.

Chambrun's smile was bitter. "Psychiatrists and analysts are getting rich on the indelible memories we have of what happened to us when we were five years old — even younger."

"Where did the name Cleaves come from?" I asked.

Chambrun shrugged. It is the only

Gallic mannerism he has. "The war was over, the Germans were gone. Collaboration was forgotten or forgiven. People had been under terrible pressure, everyone said. St. Germaine's widow married an Englishman named Harrison Cleaves, a shipping magnate. The boy, St. Germaine's son Richard, took his stepfather's name. According to George Battle he hasn't forgotten what happened to his father and has spent his adult life hating us and dreaming of retribution in some fashion."

"I don't get it," I said. "You said at the start that that afraid-of-his-own-shadow creep upstairs had paid for the rope that hanged St. Germaine."

"You must learn not to judge a package by its wrapping, Mark," Chambrun said. "George Battle is afraid of germs, he's afraid of public transportation — yes, he's afraid of his own shadow. But mostly he's afraid of vengeance."

"I still don't get it."

"You don't get to be a multi-billionaire by kissing babies," Chambrun said. "George was born rich, but only modestly rich. He turned a minor fortune into a colossus of wealth and power by being one of the toughest, most devious, most ruthless men alive today. What lies behind him is a path strewn with the crippled and dead who got in the way of his gigantic steam roller. What George fears most is that someone who survived may try to even what to him is a small and meaningless score."

"You said he 'paid for the rope'," I persisted. "If he helped you, he evidently supported some good causes."

"If what we did was a good cause," Chambrun said.

"Did he support the Resistance?"

"Yes. With money, with arms made in other countries, with influence he could bring to bear in other parts of the world."

"So his impulses were good."

Chambrun smiled that bitter smile.

"Perhaps they were good, certainly they paid off."

"How do you mean?"

"There were hundreds of men in a restored France who felt they owed him a debt. He made a great, great deal of money out of their gratitude."

"He gave you the management of the Beaumont, and the penthouse," Ruysdale said. "He must have owed you something."

I wouldn't have dared say such a thing. Chambrun looked at her as though he was pleased she'd had the courage.

"He owes me his life," Chambrun said. "I've saved it at least twice. It seems I'm to be required to save it again."

"Then you owe him something," Ruysdale said.

"He paid for the rope," Chambrun said.

"There is one thing, Mr. Chambrun," Shelda said.

"Yes?"

"It couldn't have been Richard Cleaves who fired that shot at Mr. Battle tonight. I was with him when it happened."

"With *him*!" I said.

"I had dinner with David Loring," Shelda said, ignoring me. "The other guests were Angela Adams and Mr. Cleaves. We were all together at the time the attack on Mr. Battle was made."

Chambrun nodded, a faraway look in his eyes. "The finger that squeezes the trigger isn't necessarily attached to the brain that plans the action," he said.

★ ★ ★

We had one piece of luck in that strange evening. The man assigned to the case by Homicide was Lieutenant Hardy, an old friend who'd been involved with us before. Hardy is a big, blond man who looks more like a professional football player than a detective. "Shaggy dog," were Ruysdale's words for him. He appeared to be a slow-moving, slow-thinking gent until you got to know him. The key to his success as a homicide man was thoroughness. He checks and checks and double-checks every detail of a case. He never gives up, and he will follow every clue, no matter how tenuous, until it pays off or checks out. He doesn't follow the most likely leads; he follows all the leads. You know, when he handles a case, that nothing will be overlooked. He and Chambrun have a mutual admiration society going. Chambrun, mercurial, jumps from mountain peak to mountain peak. Hardy follows, but by going down into the valley and climbing up the other side. He came into the office, looking a little ruffled but not really disturbed, just after Chambrun had made his remark about trigger fingers and detached brains. He might even have heard it from Ruysdale's office.

"So you're at it again," he said to Chambrun, "making work for me." He gave the rest of us a casual salute.

"Welcome to our city," Chambrun said, grinning at him. "Have you been upstairs?"

"Have I been upstairs!" Hardy said. He glanced at the Turkish coffeemaker on the sideboard, then at Ruysdale. "You don't have any decent drinking coffee, do you, Miss Ruysdale?" He'd had experience with the thick, strong brew from the sideboard.

"If you can drink instant," Ruysdale said, and went off to her own office and her own equipment.

Hardy sat down in a big armchair facing Chambrun's desk. "I had a call from my great white father, the mayor, telling me that I must do everything possible to insure the safety of your great white father upstairs," he said. "Trouble is I can't talk to the only witness in the case. Your Mr. Battle saw the gunman, but it will be several hours before he comes out of the shot Dr. Cobb gave him. So while I waited I thought I'd come down and go over Jerry Dodd's theory with you."

"That I was actually the target?" Chambrun asked.

"Does it add up?" Hardy asked. He took a charred-looking black pipe from his pocket and began to fill it from an oilskin pouch. Chambrun didn't answer till Hardy had his pipe going by way of a battered Zippo lighter.

"It's a theory," Chambrun said.

"You know someone who would like to do you in so elaborately?" Hardy asked. "I mean, there are twenty places in this hotel where it would be easier to get at you than that penthouse. And what luck he had, getting by three sentries, one bodyguard, and three other people bedded down in the place."

"Marvelous luck," Chambrun said.

The two of them smirked at each other like a couple of old biddies gossiping over the back fence. They enjoyed each other.

"Mostly, when you ask a man if he knows someone who wants to kill him," Hardy said, "he says 'No', or, 'Well, there is this John Smith'. I heard a name dropped as I came in; someone who couldn't have done it."

"Richard Cleaves couldn't have done it," Chambrun said. "Shelda has provided him with an alibi."

Hardy glanced at Shelda. "Maybe she's in love with him. Maybe his alibi won't hold up. I'll check it out." He meant it as a joke and he clearly thought it was quite funny.

"Let's get serious, friend, because it's going to be a long night," Chambrun said. "A man like George Battle has enemies all around the globe. It's very unpopular these days to be as rich as George Battle is."

"You don't get that way by passing out free liquor," Hardy said.

"Thirty years ago I had enemies," Chambrun said, his voice gone cold. "I lived for a good many years expecting to meet an assassin down some dark corridor. It never happened. Tonight I find that the son of a man I had killed thirty years ago — who was five years old at the time — is a guest in the hotel. This man has a reason to hate George Battle, who was an ally of mine thirty years ago. But he didn't fire the shot that lodged in the headboard of my bed. He was having what I hope was an intellectual conversation about films with Shelda."

"But as you said as I was coming in, he could have arranged to have it fired. That's the fashion of the day. You can get a man killed today for a very few dollars."

"There are undoubtedly a great many people," Chambrun said, by-passing Hardy's comment, "who have come to hate me quite a lot over the years I have run this hotel. There are people whose credit I've cut off, there are the wives of double-crossing husbands I've covered for, there are mobsters who have tried to look respectable by registering here and who got kicked out by me, and there are perhaps three dozen widely assorted employees — ex-employees: waiters, bartenders, chefs, housemaids, bell boys, cleaning people, office help whom I've fired for slovenly work or for trying to steal from me. Murderous hatred? I doubt it. Of course somebody can have blown his stack."

"So you don't think with Jerry that it was meant for you?"

"It could have been," Chambrun said.

"But you think it's more likely it was meant for Battle?"

Chambrun watched the smoke curl up from his cigarette. "There are some interesting questions for you to answer, Lieutenant," he said. "If it was meant for George why, after managing to get past the sentries, the bodyguard, Dr. Cobb and the two servants, did our killer only fire one shot that missed? Jerry guesses a thirty-eight police special. He could have fired four, five shots. Why didn't he go on shooting when he saw he had missed?"

"Maybe he had only one shell in the gun."

"Plan so carefully and come unprepared?"

"Maybe he just wanted to scare Battle," Hardy said.

"Run all those risks just to scare him?" Chambrun shook his head. "Let me tell you one thing about George Battle. He has allowed people to believe that he is a timid, frightened man. He's helped to create that belief. But when it comes to real danger, he's got the guts of a burglar. Maybe that isn't quite accurate, come to think of it. Maybe it's that he's so afraid of dying that he will run any kind of risk to stay alive."

"Maybe it was just meant as a warning," Hardy said.

"Quite possible. Even probably," Chambrun said.

"But was it meant for you or was it meant for Battle?"

"Let's consider something unrelated

to that question," Chambrun said. "The elevator to the penthouse was restricted to people okayed by Battle. The fire stairs were bolted on the inside. He couldn't have come over the roof. I've said I'd trust Jerry and his men with my life."

Hardy's eyes widened. "Are you saying nobody got into the penthouse from outside?"

"I'm asking the question," Chambrun said.

Hardy stood up abruptly. "So he may be up there right now with the guy who took a shot at him."

"He should be safe enough with all your crew up there," Chambrun said. "But if I were you, Lieutenant, I'd certainly like to talk to Butler, the bodyguard, Allerton, the manservant, Gaston, the chef — and Dr. Cobb. And George, when he comes to."

Hardy left quickly for a big man.

It had come a little fast for me to take in. "You're just trying to get him off your back," I said. "You don't believe for a minute one of those four guys took a shot at Battle. They're the people he trusts."

"Judas was also trusted," Chambrun said.

4

IN theory the people who work for the Beaumont are committed to silence about anything that goes wrong with its routines. A violence can be the beginning of a kind of panic if the word spreads among our hundreds of transient guests. Get hundreds of people making hysterical inquiries at the switchboard and our whole telephone system is disrupted; dozens of people will want to check out at once, jamming up our front desk and our bookkeeping department, demanding to get their precious belongings out of our safety deposit boxes. It can generate a madhouse that will continue long after whatever the trouble is has been cleared up.

Perhaps it was asking too much that the attack on George Battle could have been kept a secret. The lobby, normally quiet at ten o'clock at night, had still been crowded with ladies hoping to get a glimpse of David Loring. The police had not sneaked into the hotel when they came. Ten minutes after they arrived, the word had spread like a forest fire. There was no time or reason to check out who had started the story going. Dozens of people on the staff knew that George Battle was in the penthouse and that extraordinary precautions were being taken to protect him, and when those precautions broke down, so did any secrecy about it. The minute the story was out, literally hundreds of reporters, photographers, and feature writers from the press, radio, and television were storming the hotel. Someone had to deal with them, and that turned out to be my job.

It was after one o'clock in the morning when I finally found myself facing the news corps in one of the private dining rooms on the main floor. They weren't a happy family. They'd been kept without any information for a couple of hours. All they had was rumor.

I made a short statement. "Someone broke into the penthouse where Mr. Battle is staying and took a shot at him. The shot missed. Mr. Battle is unhurt, though in shock and unable to make a statement. As yet the police haven't identified the gunman. He apparently got away in the immediate confusion that followed the firing of the shot. That's all I can tell you, ladies and gentlemen."

It wasn't enough.

"We understand special precautions were being taken to protect Mr. Battle. Why?"

"The precautions were not special for a man of Mr. Battle's importance," I said.

"Sentries on the roof, an armed guard outside his bedroom door; that isn't special?"

The word was certainly out. "Not special," I said.

"He expected some kind of attack?"

I tried to keep it light. "Not the kind that happened. He expected some of you people might go to any lengths to get an interview with him. He was tired. He wanted to get some sleep."

"Why don't you level with us, Haskell?" It was a young reporter from the *News* whom I knew well. "We know Battle lives in fear of his life — the way he travels, the constant protection. What instructions did the sentries and the bodyguard really have?"

"To keep out intruders."

"What is Battle doing here in America? He hasn't been here for nearly twenty years."

"Seventeen," I said.

"Why is he here?"

"He has a right to come and go," I said. "This is a free country."

"We can argue that some other time," my friend from the *News* said. "He must have had a special reason for making this trip. Two yachts, for God sake. It must have cost him a half a million dollars just to make the trip."

87

"I understand he may be interested in financing a film," I said, and instantly wished I hadn't.

"Maxie Zorn's epic?" My friend from the *News* grinned at me. "Is it true your ex-girl friend is going to play a nude scene with David Loring?"

"I don't think any casting decisions, beyond David Loring, have been made," I said.

"You hope!" my friend said.

"I don't have any more information for you, ladies and gentlemen," I said. "The police will have to answer questions about the attempted crime. Mr. Battle is under sedation and I have no authorization to make any kind of statement for him. You'll just have to wait for anything more. I promise to cooperate with you as best I can."

They weren't happy, and I knew they were going to be milling around the hotel for the rest of the night, but there wasn't anything more I could do for them.

The Trapeze Bar was still open and

I decided to go up there for a drink. The Trapeze Bar is almost literally suspended in space in the foyer to the Grand Ballroom. The walls are iron grillwork, and some artist of the Calder school has decorated it with a collection of mobiles of circus performers operating on trapezes. The faint circulation of air from a conditioner keeps these little figures in constant motion.

Ordinarily the customers have begun to thin out at this time of night, but not now. It was crowded to the doors and the ordinary gentle hum of voices was now a loud, excited noisiness. I was about to turn away when I saw Eddie, the bartender, signal to me that there was an empty stool at the bar. It wasn't until I slid onto it that I saw that my neighbor on the left was Peter Potter, Maxie Zorn's deformed little PR man.

"Been saving this for you," he said. "I guessed you'd show up, sooner or later." His head and shoulders came just above the edge of the bar, his short little legs dangled in space. "I don't do well at press conferences without a periscope." He held out his hand. His grip was firm. "I'm Peter Potter."

"I know," I said.

"I dream you'll give me the real lowdown," he said.

I signaled to Eddie for my usual, a double Jack Daniels on the rocks. "It seems that most people in the hotel know more about it than I do," I said.

"I understand the clumsy assassin wore a stocking mask," Potter said. "Unrecognizable. I hope to God he was over four feet tall."

"I think it would have been mentioned if he hadn't been," I said. "Otherwise you think you might be a suspect?"

"Why not? I hate the sonofabitch."

"George Battle?"

"I hate all big, powerful men," Potter said. "Unfortunately the best I can do about it is a kick in the shins or a bite out of the calf of a leg." His smile was winning. He didn't seem to be really hating anyone. "My job, however, requires me to be concerned about Battle. Seven million bucks' worth of financing is at stake."

"So I've heard."

"And you may be the key to it."

"I?"

"Of course," he said, his smile widening. "Your girl."

"I don't have a girl," I said.

"Oh, come, Haskell. Your ex-girl, then. The lovely Shelda."

"I have no control over what she does," I said.

"Want to bet?"

"You know something I don't know?" I asked.

"I always know something other people don't know," Potter said. "It's the only way I can keep from being overlooked."

"I doubt that."

"Oh, people stare at me," he said, and now there was bitterness in his voice. "They laugh at me or feel pity for me. Which is your inclination, chum?"

It was a nasty question. "I haven't made up my mind," I said. "Maybe neither. What do you know that I don't know?"

"About what?"

"About Shelda."

"Ah, yes, Shelda. A complicated decision she has to make. Modesty versus a small fortune. You know something? There's only one thing I can think of I wouldn't do for a small fortune. I wouldn't appear naked in front of anyone. But if I were beautiful, like Shelda, it would be a simple decision. I'd be rich, and admired, and quickly forgotten if I wanted to be forgotten."

"The thing is, would she forget — afterwards?" I said.

Potter's warm brown eyes looked at me quite seriously. "If she can't forget, you're lost anyway, chum."

"You suggested you know something I don't know — something that might give me some control in the situation."

"She loves you," Potter said.

"Nonsense! What makes you think so?"

"Because she denies it so vehemently," he said. "Let me put some cards face up on the table for you, Haskell. Maxie Zorn is desperate. He has but big money troubles. If he doesn't find the money to make this film and when he does if it isn't a big success, Maxie is done for. But it's not just Maxie, but hundreds of people who work for him — office staff, technical staff, the whole barrelful that go to make up a production unit. Maxie was outraged when Battle made your Shelda a condition — until he saw Shelda. Now he'd be delighted to use her. His main problem, in addition to Shelda's hesitation, is Loring. Our David doesn't want Shelda for the part, though he's been a good boy and asked her to do it."

"Why doesn't he want her?" I asked.

Potter laughed. "No way to make

it right for you, is there, chum? If we want her, we're villains; if we don't want her, we're villains. Loring wants his girl friend, Angela, for the part. Now we come to a kind of a puzzle. Why does Battle make her a condition of financing this film? Maxie doesn't care why. It fascinates me. Maxie thinks he has a lech for her and can't make it himself, so he wants to be a voyeur by way of seven minutes of film. I don't think so. You see, I know George Battle. I worked for him once."

"You worked for him?"

Potter nodded. "Most devious mind you ever encountered. There's never a simple answer to why he does anything. The simple answer to this thing with Shelda is that he's a dirty old man. It's so simple that it can't be so. Do you know what I did for him in Europe for almost a year? You couldn't guess. I was a secret messenger for him — carrying life-and-death communications to industrial and political allies of his. Now I ask you, Haskell, would you hire me to be a secret messenger?"

"Why not? You're obviously a clever man."

"Sure I'm clever, but there's one thing I can't do. I can't disguise myself. I'm four feet tall. I have a hump on my back that won't go away. If I want someone to carry a secret for me, I hire a man who would be anonymous, who can disappear into a crowd, who can change his identity if necessary. But George Battle hired me, perhaps the most easily followed man in the whole world. Oh, I was followed. I spent a year trying to duck away from and escape men who were trained in the art of surveillance. Every time I led them straight to the person I was supposed to be delivering my message to. I told Battle I was a failure, but he just smiled and said I was doing fine. Then, one day, I was taking a message to a man in Prague. It was a thick, sealed envelope. One night I was in a hotel room, after trying to shake a tail all day. What can be so important? I asked myself. So I steamed open the envelope. Want to guess what was in it? Never mind, I'll tell you. Blank paper! Oh, no invisible ink or any crap like that. Just blank paper. I knew then what the game was. The best industrial spies in Europe had been following me all over the map, while the real messenger with the real messages was doing his job unhampered, and George Battle was laughing himself sick. I quit. I was getting paid a thousand dollars a week, but I quit."

"Why?"

"Because he was using my deformity to play a joke on his business enemies," Potter said. He took a sip of the brandy in front of him on the bar. "But, enough of my personal sensitivities. Why does the master mind want your Shelda in the film? Seven million dollars to look at a film clip of a pretty secretary in the raw? Never! He can hire a parade of broads to walk past him naked for twenty-four hours a day for a great deal less than that. So what's the answer? Nothing he does is for any obvious reason." Potter grinned at me. "You can't imagine anyone not wanting to look at your girl without her clothes on, but I assure you Battle has far too many irons in the fire to waste time on that kind of vicarious thrill. So why?"

"If you're right, I don't know why," I said.

"He's one of the shrewdest men in the world about people," Potter said. "He knows exactly what to expect of them. Your Shelda has been working for him for a year, I understand. I promise you he knows all there is to know about her. So he must have known that she wouldn't jump at the chance, even with a big chunk of money involved. And she didn't. Also, may I point out to you that it was he who made the suggestion that perhaps she ought to talk to you about it on the assumption, he told Maxie, that you would take a practical view of it."

"He didn't know me," I said.

"Let's not be too sure," Potter said. "Shelda has worked for him for a year. There must have been some moments of casual chit-chat. Isn't it true that he offered her a job as a favor to Chambrun — because you and she needed to be separated for a while? Don't look so surprised. Shelda told me that herself. SO, I say Battle may have made a very sound evaluation of you. He knew you would say 'no' at the top of your lungs if Shelda asked you. So what can we conclude? That Shelda was thrown into the ball game for purposes of stalling."

"That doesn't make any sense," I said. "He wouldn't need excuses for delaying a decision to finance the film."

"No?" Potter lifted his brandy glass and squinted at its dark dregs. "Unless, to mix metaphors, somebody has him by the short hairs and he needs time to wriggle off the hook." He put down his glass and laughed. "You want to start a panic, chum? Get Shelda to say yes, now, tonight. I'll bet you the best dinner this fancy joint can provide that Mr. George Battle wakes right up out of his drugged sleep screaming." He slid down off the bar stool and looked up at me, his brown eyes twinkling. "Cheerio, chum. If you come up with a better theory than mine, let me know."

* * *

I felt suddenly dog tired. Wheels within wheels. I knew one thing. I had to talk to Shelda or I wasn't going to get much sleep, tired or not. I wanted to start over with her. I wanted her to forget all the jibes and juvenile cracks I'd made. I wanted her.

I went to the house phone in the far corner of the Trapeze and asked the switchboard to connect me with her room. No answer. I'd left her in Chambrun's office with the boss and Ruysdale and I headed back there in the hope she was still there. I found her in the outer office with Ruysdale.

"Wondered when you'd be back," Ruysdale said. She looked as fresh as if she'd just gotten up from ten hours' sleep. "How are the fourth estate?"

"Churning," I said. "I suppose I ought to report to the boss."

"He's gone back up to the penthouse. No instructions for you," Ruysdale said. She stood up and walked toward the door to the inner sanctum. She smiled at us. "I'd better make a fresh batch of Turkish swamp water."

Shelda was looking down at the toe of that damned shoe again.

"I'd like to apologize for being such a schmuk," I said.

She looked up at me slowly. "Oh, Mark!" she said.

Believe it or not, that's all there was to it. She was suddenly in my arms and the beloved mouth was pressed against mine and I held her and held her. Eventually we separated to look at each other and she was laughing and crying.

"I thought you'd never say anything nice," she said.

"I think I am madly, insanely in love with you," I said.

"Whatever you want I want," she said.

"My place," I said.

We turned to the door, my arm around her — and Ruysdale reappeared, frowning.

"I'm sorry, Mark, but I may need you," she said.

"Not now, baby. Not for God sake now," I said.

Ruysdale was headed for her telephone. "Mr. Kranepool, the assistant district attorney in charge upstairs, called about a half hour ago and asked Mr. Chambrun to come upstairs. Mr. Chambrun left immediately. Now Mr. Kranepool calls and asks Mr. Chambrun to come upstairs. I tell him he responded to the first call half an hour ago. Mr. Kranepool says there never was a first call." She got a connection on the phone and spoke with Mrs. Kiley, the night supervisor on the switchboard. "There was a call for Mr. Chambrun about a half hour ago from the penthouse, Mrs. Kiley. Will you check it for me?" She covered the mouthpiece with her hand. "They're monitoring all calls in and out of the penthouse." Then Mrs. Kiley evidently came back on and Ruysdale's frown deepened. "Thank you, Mrs. Kiley." She put down the phone and looked at me, and I thought there was something like fear in her eyes. "There's been no call from the penthouse until just now. The call half an hour ago came from an outside phone."

"The first call was a phony," I said.

Ruysdale nodded. "Take that other phone, Mark, call the penthouse and get Jerry Dodd down here on the double." She asked the switchboard to get her the room Chambrun was occupying while Battle had the penthouse. "Not that I think he's there," she muttered.

I had some trouble getting Jerry

on the line, but he came on at last, sounding irritated. "It better be important," he said. "Where the hell is the boss?"

I told him about the fake phone call from Kranepool and that Chambrun had taken off half an hour ago.

"Could he have gone to his temporary quarters?" Jerry's voice was hard and cold. I glanced at Ruysdale. She was shaking her head at me. No answer from Chambrun's room. I told Jerry.

"Jesus! He wouldn't listen to me," Jerry said.

Part Two

1

YOU have to bear in mind that, to me, Chambrun was a kind of superman. He was also a cantankerous taskmaster as far as the Beaumont was concerned. Nothing happens to superman, but a perfectionist like the Great Man could be sidetracked if he saw something going wrong with the Swiss-watch workings of the hotel. Things were going wrong that night, like the invasion of the Spartan Bar by David Loring's female admirers. I refused to be panicked in spite of the butterflies that were flapping around in my stomach. I could visualize the boss downstairs, driving the ladies out of the Spartan and raising general hell with the main floor staff, including Mike Maggio, the night bell captain. You didn't let things get out of hand at the Beaumont, and someone had.

It wasn't an illogical idea. "If he was going to the penthouse, he might have gone down to the lobby to get the one elevator that goes to the roof," I said to Ruysdale and Shelda. Shelda was holding tightly to my hand and I felt strong and tall and manly! "Things are kind of screwed up downstairs, and you know the boss."

Ruysdale nodded, as if she were only half listening. "I know the boss," she said. "His first concern tonight is what's going on in the penthouse. If he went through the lobby and saw something wrong, he'd make a note of it, but he wouldn't have let himself be sidetracked. He thought Kranepool had sent for him."

I couldn't get it through my head that Chambrun could be made to do something he didn't want to do. I couldn't believe that any kind of violent thing could have happened to him; not in the Beaumont, not in the place he controlled so effectively.

And yet someone had broken through security and fired a shot at a man in his bed earlier that night. If that had been an inside job — one of Battle's four trusties — as Chambrun had suggested, then Chambrun was in no danger from them. They had known who was in the bed.

"The Battle case is what he's concerned with, I'll admit," I said. "Maybe he stumbled on something connected with it. Maybe he ran into Richard Cleaves or someone else he knows who might be involved. He would let himself be sidetracked, wouldn't he, if he thought he was onto something important?"

Ruysdale didn't answer. I knew I was fishing for comforting answers. She was way ahead of me, assuming the worst, and moving to face it. She was at the phone again, asking Karl Nevers, the night manager, and Mike Maggio, the night bell captain, to come up to the office at once.

Then Jerry Dodd was with us. His

bright eyes asked a question without words.

"Nothing," Ruysdale said in a flat voice.

"What about that first phone call?" Jerry asked.

"I took it," Ruysdale said. "An unfamiliar male voice said he was Lester Kranepool, the assistant D.A., and would Mr. Chambrun come up to the penthouse at once."

"You don't know Kranepool?"

"Never heard of him until tonight," Ruysdale said. "I've never seen him or spoken to him until he phoned."

"Except that wasn't Kranepool," Jerry said. "Damn! One thing's for sure. The boss wouldn't leave the hotel voluntarily without letting you know, Betsy — letting some one of us know."

"That's for sure," Ruysdale said. "Let's face it, Jerry. There's nothing voluntary about what's happened to him."

"If there is, I'll break his goddam

neck," Jerry said.

There was no one with the title of Assistant Manager at the Beaumont. I knew why in the next few minutes. Ruysdale was the boss's stand-in, with every detail of the operation at her fingertips. While Jerry Dodd used one phone to call his best people into immediate action, Ruysdale was calmly alerting the top people on the hotel staff that we had an emergency. The hotel must continue to operate as though nothing had happened. There mustn't be a hint that anything had happened to Chambrun. If he wasn't back on the job when the next day's business began, the word must be that he was simply out of the office for personal reasons for a few hours. She, Ruysdale, would make any emergency decisions that had to be made, and if anyone doubted her authority, she had special orders from the boss in writing. I don't think anyone would have questioned her.

Art Stein and a couple of others of Jerry's security men showed up while the phone calls were being made.

Jerry finally gave it to them straight. "There are several possibilities," he told them. "The first and most unlikely for my money is that the boss has left the hotel of his own free will. He stumbled on something, probably relating to the Battle case, and it took him away without giving him time to notify us. Or, having been lured out of here by a phony phone call, he was persuaded to go somewhere, willingly, without telling us. He's been gone about fifty-five minutes now. Ordinarily you don't think a man is missing when you haven't seen him for fifty-five minutes. It's different in this case."

"You still think that shot upstairs may have been meant for Mr. Chambrun?" Stein asked.

"I do. Maybe more than ever now. They didn't get him one way they try another."

I felt Shelda's hand tighten in mine.

"So he was suckered into a trap," Stein said.

"That's almost certain," Jerry said. "First possibility is they took him somewhere and are holding him, maybe for ransom which we'll hear about, maybe for something worse that I don't want to think about. Second possibility, it was all over fast. They knifed him, clubbed him — the body is not very far away, in a broom closet, down one of the elevator shafts, in one of the cellar areas."

I glanced at Ruysdale. Her face was a pale mask.

"I figure the way that could have happened would be either just outside here in the hall, or in an elevator on the way up. So first we look for a body, hopefully still alive."

"It would be hard for anyone to carry him out of the hotel," Stein said, "and I can't imagine the boss letting himself be taken."

"Not with a gun in his back?" Jerry asked.

"He'd have been seen," Stein said. "You'd have heard, now that you've started asking."

"He could have gotten out if he didn't want to be seen," Ruysdale said. "He's done it hundreds of times, don't ask me how."

"But he wouldn't show somebody how to take him out," Stein said.

"He might," Ruysdale said. "He'd be very tough to handle if the danger was just to him. But if someone else was threatened — Mr. Battle, or you, Jerry, or Mark. Or me." She looked away.

"So first we go over the hotel like a vacuum cleaner," Jerry said. "Then, God help us, there isn't any kind of a lead to anything."

"Oh, I think there's a lead, Jerry," Ruysdale said. "It would be too wildly coincidental if it didn't have something to do with Mr. Battle's presence here in the hotel. Mr. Chambrun has known Mr. Battle for more than thirty years. He knows more about him than perhaps anyone else. Someone may think Mr.

Chambrun has the key to a great deal of money. There are not millions, but several billion dollars represented in that penthouse — industrial power, political power."

"And the crazy sonofabitch is slugged out with a sedative when so many people want to talk to him," Jerry said.

"There is one person it might be worth talking to while you wait for him to wake up," I said. "Like Chambrun said, you don't have to have pulled the trigger to be responsible. Richard Cleaves apparently hates both Battle and the boss."

"So you and I will go and talk to him," Jerry said. "Get moving, Art. I want every square inch of this hotel covered."

"It's a long job, Jerry."

"Let's hope you don't have to finish it," Jerry said. He beckoned to me, taking it for granted I was with him.

I looked at Shelda.

"You have to go, darling," she said.

My girl!

Just outside the office door is the bank of elevators. The wall opposite is the outside wall of the building. Behind the elevators is the lobby, an open space rising three stories high. The second floor, then, is a corridor facing the elevators, with Chambrun's offices ballooning out on one end and on the other, the bookkeeping offices, the switchboards, my apartment and my office. East of the elevators is a wide, open stairway leading down to the lobby. There is a fire stair next to the bookkeeping offices. Those are the only two exits from the second floor except the elevators, four of them.

Jerry and I stood by the elevators, looking up and down the corridor, not speaking. Each of us, I guess, was trying to imagine what had happened out here. Chambrun had been summoned, he believed, to the penthouse. There would have been three possible things he could have done. He could have walked down the open stair into the lobby and taken

116

the one elevator that went up all the way to the roof. He could have taken one of the other elevators down to the lobby. That would, I thought, have been out of character unless the car was standing right there with the door open. He was a much too impatient man to wait for a car to take him one flight down. The third possibility was that he had taken an up-elevator to the twenty-fourth floor, planning to change elevators there.

"The guys who suckered him out of his office couldn't gamble on what he'd do," Jerry said. "They have to meet him right here, head on. They couldn't risk the lobby, where a hundred people would see whatever happened, or the twenty-fourth floor, where cops are seeing to it that no one gets up to the roof."

"They waited for him in the elevator that goes to the roof?"

Jerry shook his head. "Elevator operator and a cop in that car," he said. "First question I asked when I came down from the penthouse was whether they'd seen him."

You should know that all the elevators at the Beaumont have operators from seven o'clock in the morning until midnight. The rest of the time they are self-service. There'd have been no employee on the regular elevators at the time Chambrun had left his office.

We walked down the open stairway to the lobby. Things had quieted down there. The Spartan Bar had closed for the night and the lady invaders had reluctantly left. The Blue Lagoon, the hotel's night club which opens off the far end of the lobby, had also closed. The Trapeze Bar, overhead, was dark.

Mike Maggio, the night bell captain, saw us and came hurrying over. Mike is a handsome, dark Italian with a normally mischievous grin. There was something almost comical about the seriousness of his face now.

"I was just on my way up to the office," he told Jerry. "When I got the word from Miss Ruysdale, I wanted to check out as well as I could down here first. Nobody saw him, Jerry. I swear I would have. I was afraid he'd show while those broads were raising hell in the Spartan, and I kept looking for him, wondering what I'd say to him."

"You better get your orders from Ruysdale," Jerry said, "but keep asking. Don't make it sound like anything's happened; just say he's needed and we don't know where he is."

"Will do," Mike said. "You think it's bad, Jerry?"

"I think it's bad," Jerry said.

The lobby had a strange feel for me. This place was my home; I lived here, I worked here, I found most of my recreation here. In spite of its great size I think I would have noticed any small thing out of place, any routine not running normally. The lobby seemed perfectly normal now, and yet it felt wrong. I suddenly realized what it was. At all times, no matter what the problems, the complaints, the irritating confrontations with irritating guests to whom you had to be polite, the fashion people, the society mothers demanding perfection for their 'coming-out' daughters, the press agents for important people and for people who wanted to be important, there was the inner assurance that no problem was too tough to solve because God was in his heaven — on the second floor — and all was right with the world. Now God wasn't there, and not even Betsy Ruysdale could fill the void. The Captain wasn't on the bridge; the coach had left the team to improvise its own game plan. I knew, as Jerry and I took the elevator to the fourteenth floor, how much we depended on Chambrun, and that the simple knowledge that he wasn't there made us — or me at least — feel curiously incompetent.

Outside the door of Richard Cleaves' room I glanced at my watch. It was a quarter past two. He'd probably be in bed, very much annoyed by our intrusion.

He wasn't in bed, but his annoyance

was electric. He opened the door and stood looking at us, black glasses hiding his eyes. He was wearing slacks and a white shirt, sleeves rolled up to reveal muscular, tanned arms. He reminded me a little of George Peppard, the actor.

"Yes?" he said. A cold voice, a hostile voice.

"I'm Dodd, the hotel's security officer," Jerry said. "This is Mr. Haskell, the hotel's public relations director. We'd like to talk to you, Mr. Cleaves."

"Not tonight," Cleaves said. He started to close the door, but Jerry's foot was in the way. The hall light glittered against the black glasses. "Get your foot out of the door, Dodd, unless you want it broken."

I was mildly amused. I'd seen Jerry handle belligerent drunks twice his size. The aggressive Mr. Cleaves wasn't going to intimidate him. There's something enjoyable about watching a little guy handle a big guy.

"I can get a cop down here in about five minutes to arrest you," Jerry said, "or we can talk nice and friendly."

Cleaves made a right judgment. He didn't try to break Jerry's foot. "What is it you want to talk about?"

"An attempted murder, possibly two," Jerry said.

I thought I'd try something direct. "We know something about your history, Mr. Cleaves."

"If you do," he said, "you know I regret George Battle didn't get it right between the eyes."

"And what do you hope has happened to Chambrun?" Jerry asked, his foot still in the door.

"What has happened to him?" Cleaves asked.

"That's what we're here to ask you."

I was watching his face. It's hard to guess what a man is thinking when you can't see his eyes, but I could have sworn he was surprised. There was a little intake of breath, a little twitch at the corners of his hidden eyes.

122

"You've hooked me, gentlemen," Cleaves said. "Come in and tell us what you're talking about." He stepped back from the door.

"Us" turned out to be David Loring and the glamorous Miss Angela Adams. Cleaves had a sitting room-bedroom suite, and the actor and his lady were sitting on a couch, side by side. On a coffee table in front of them were a variety of bottles — Scotch, vodka, brandy. There was an ice bucket, glasses, a couple of the Beaumont's silver stirrers. Ash trays were full. I saw Jerry take that all in.

"How long have you been here, Mr. Loring?" he asked.

"Just a minute," Cleaves said. "You don't have to answer any questions, David. This is just the house dick."

It's strange to meet someone like Loring whom you've seen a hundred times on the screen. You feel as if you knew him and you don't know him at all. His one-sided little smile was familiar, the way he cocked his head to one side was familiar, the very direct look in his dark blue eyes was familiar, the husky speech with the slightly British sound to it was familiar.

"Miss Adams and I have been drinking with Richard since a little before midnight," he said. "So I think you should bear in mind, Mr. Housedick, that we are all a little potted and therefore not entirely reliable."

The gorgeous Miss Adams was leaning back, her arms spread out on either side of the back of the couch. This tended to reveal a rather stimulating amount of bare bosom. Her eyes were narrowed, watching me, as if she was daring me to let my mouth drop open. There was a zipper in the front of the scarlet housecoat she was wearing that would have opened it right down to the floor.

"If you three have been together since before midnight, I don't have any questions to ask you," Jerry said.

Cleaves was sweetening a Scotch on

the rocks. "You can't get away with that, Dodd," he said. His straight, hard mouth moved in a tiny smile. "You've whetted my curiosity. What has happened to Chambrun?"

"If you've all been here since before twelve, you can't help me to provide an answer to that," Jerry said. He turned toward the door.

"How about a drink?" Cleaves said, turning on charm.

"No, thanks," Jerry said.

"Maybe you feel more communicative than your friend, Haskell," Cleaves said. He gestured toward the drink table.

"Sorry," I said.

"I gather you know that I've made a life study of Mr. Battle and Mr. Chambrun. You seem worried. Let me reassure you. They are indestructible, those two. They live charmed lives. Has someone taken a shot at Mr. Chambrun and missed? That would fit the pattern?"

"What pattern?" Jerry asked.

"Things are not what they seem when you deal with Battle and Chambrun," Cleaves said. "Someone is said to have shot at Battle and missed. My life study tells me that missing is exactly what was intended. What is supposed to have happened to Chambrun? Because whatever is supposed to have happened is probably not what happened at all. That's the way the game is played."

Jerry was intrigued in spite of himself. "Mr. Chambrun gets a phone call from the assistant D.A. in the penthouse asking him to come up. He went, and has disappeared into thin air."

"How exciting," Miss Adams said in a slow, drawling voice. She moved slightly, almost exposing an entire breast.

"And the phone call turned out not to be from the D.A. at all?" Cleaves asked. He certainly knew how part of the game was played. "Any signs of violence?"

"Not yet," Jerry said.

Cleaves took a sip of his drink. "I

have every reason to regret that," he said. "I take it you know why."

"Your father," I said.

His mouth became a straight, hard slit. "Chambrun told you?"

"Yes."

"I've spent thirty years trying to convince myself that Battle and Chambrun are Siamese twins," Cleaves said. "It doesn't quite work. Chambrun was a genuine patriot. I could cut his heart out for what he did, if that kind of thing was possible for me. But I understand it. Perhaps in his shoes I'd have done the same thing. His cause, he thought, was just. He faced me with it a long time ago, when I was still in my teens. He laid it on the line without any ifs, ends, or buts. He took the entire responsibility. He left himself wide open to me. I — I spent a lot of time preparing myself for the perfect crime. You see, I don't want to die for a justified crime, gentlemen. I made myself into an expert marksman with any kind of gun." He smiled. "Rest assured, if you can break my alibi for the time Battle was shot at, I still have another alibi. I couldn't have missed at that distance." He paused a moment to light a cigarette. "In the last ten years I've had a dozen chances to settle with Chambrun. Would you believe I've looked at him five times through the sights of a gun and could never pull the trigger? Something about him, god damn him! I could have gotten away with it and I couldn't do it. Battle is something else again."

"In what way?" Jerry asked.

"In every way you can imagine," Cleaves said.

"I hate him," Angela Adams said. "Why does he insist on that girl being in David's picture?"

"Good question," Cleaves said, "because it isn't for any of the reasons that come instantly to mind. That's the key to George Battle. None of the motives he appears to have for anything he does are the real ones."

"His money is real," David Loring

said. "That's what's important to us."

"Only we haven't got it yet, so it isn't real," Cleaves said.

"You shouldn't have any trouble getting financing for your book," I said. "It's a best seller."

"If I told you that ordinary money sources have, without explanation, dried up, would you be surprised? Battle hasn't said yes to financing the film, but he hasn't said no. Would you believe that in the complex financial world in which he lives, in which he has such enormous power and influence, that the word is out that A Man's World is not to be considered until he says so?"

"It doesn't make sense," I said. "Could he make that much profit out of it?"

"In his terms the profit will be chicken feed," Cleaves said. "Have you read my book, Haskell?"

"Sorry, but I haven't gotten to it."

"I wrote it, so I must know it pretty well," Cleaves said.

"It's so wonderfully sexy," Angela Adams said. "The woman's part is just perfect for me. Why he wants that blonde tootsie who has never acted in her life is beyond me."

Cleaves allowed himself that tight smile. "Wasn't it Lord Chesterfield who said about sex that the pleasure was momentary, the price exorbitant, and the position ridiculous? What you have to sell, darling, is not so wildly extraordinary."

"Louse!" she said.

David Loring laughed and put his hand on the lady's thigh. "You are obviously speaking without experience, Richard. Let me assure you all cats are not alike in the dark."

"Angel," Angela said, and stroked his hand.

"My book isn't a sex manual," Cleaves said. "It's the story of a political assassination; someone like Robert Kennedy, killed by some juvenile crackpot at a political rally. The hero, the part we hope David will play, is the victim's brother. He doesn't believe the killer is just a psychotic kid who killed his brother for kicks. He believes it was planned by someone high up in the political power structure and that the kid was just the unbalanced instrument. People thought that about Robert Kennedy's killer, about President Kennedy's killer, about Martin Luther King's killer. It's not a new idea. In my book the hero sets out to expose the truth and finds himself suddenly the hunted and not the hunter. It's a good suspense story, it makes what I hope are some fairly shrewd comments about the power structure in our society, but there is no reason why George Battle should either like it or want to stop its being made into a film. There's no one remotely like him in the story." Cleaves laughed. "There is no one remotely like George Battle. What I have invented must seem like kindergarten stuff to him." Cleaves suddenly hit the drink table with his fist, so hard that glasses and bottles jumped. "Why has he gotten into the act? He's never financed a film before. Maxie Zorn didn't go to him for money; he came to Maxie. I said to hell with it. I didn't want him connected with my book. I didn't want him contributing to my success. I didn't want to owe the sonofabitch anything. So I went to other sources and, believe it or not as I told you, the doors were all suddenly closed."

"Battle's trying to make it up to you," Jerry suggested. "What he helped do to your father back there."

Cleaves' laugh was bitter. "He never tried to make anything up to anyone in his whole life. Nobody in the whole world matters to him except himself. Incidentally, I've never been able to get close to him except with an army of people around him. His villa in France is like a fortress. He never travels in any public way. I've never had him in the sights of a gun. If I had, I'd have had no trouble squeezing the trigger."

"Because he helped finance the

Resistance that killed your father," I said.

"It was a cause with Chambrun," Cleaves said. "With Battle it was a means for acquiring money and power. He placed his bets on the right horse — the Resistance." He shook his head slowly. "He wouldn't bother to try to make something up to me. He may be afraid of catching a heavy cold, but he's not afraid of me. There's something about my book, as a property, that concerns him. The hell of it is I wrote it, I invented it, and I don't have the vaguest notion what it can be."

"Interesting parlor game," Jerry said, "but I'm looking for a missing man." He started for the door again.

"Ask Battle," Cleaves said. "It's a hundred-to-one he can tell you exactly where Chambrun is. He knows everything that goes on in this godforsaken world."

2

"**W**HEN you hate someone, you can really build him into a monster," Jerry said, as we walked along the corridor toward the elevators.

I was thinking that the story I'd had from Potter went right along with what we'd heard from Cleaves. "Nothing you know about Battle or you hear about him, true or false, makes him very much like anyone you've heard about before," I said.

"Just remember something, Buster," Jerry said, giving me an angry look. "Battle is the boss's friend; he's the boss's boss. He can have two heads for all I care. Chambrun wants him safe and that's the way we're going to keep him."

From a house phone near the elevators Jerry checked with his people.

No sign of Chambrun, alive or dead. No leads. Nobody had seen anything.

"Let's see how Hardy is doing," Jerry said.

Getting from the twenty-fourth floor to the roof was like trying to break into Fort Knox. The horse was gone, so to speak, but the cops really had the stable locked now. Finally word came down from Hardy that we were permitted to come up to the penthouse.

The law was still stalled up there. Apparently no one had gotten to the bedroom yet, where they hoped to find fingerprints, to dig the bullet out of the headboard so it could be submitted to ballistics, to question the sleeping George Battle. Dr. Cobb had, so far, held the fort, it seemed. He was sitting on the couch in the living room, looking exhausted. A cigarette dangled between his flabby lips, and a little drool of saliva ran out of one corner of his mouth.

A dark, intense young man in a nicely tailored blue suit was not letting the doctor relax. I guessed this was Kranepool, the assistant D.A.

"There has to be something you can give him that will bring him to, Doctor," he was saying as we came in. "We can't stall any longer. Either he can be waked, or he's so far gone we can work around him."

The doctor shook his head, mechanically, from side to side. Cigarette ash dribbled down the front of his dressing gown.

Kranepool was diverted by our arrival. "Anything?" he asked Jerry.

"Not yet."

"You able to trace the call that was supposed to have come from me?"

"Only that it was made on an outside phone."

"What do you mean? Outside the hotel?"

"No. Just not a phone that connects directly with the switchboard; not a room phone, not a house phone. There are fifty pay phones scattered around the hotel. Most of the co-ops, like this, have their own lines in addition to a house phone." He gestured. "That phone on the end table is an outside line. The one on the sideboard is a house phone."

"What are you doing to find Chambrun?" Kranepool asked.

"Looking," Jerry said, and turned away. I had a feeling he didn't like bright young men in authority at that moment. "Where's Lieutenant Hardy?"

"Guest bedroom," Kranepool said. "He's questioning the help." He turned back to Dr. Cobb. "Now, for the last time, Doctor — "

Jerry and I went down the hall to the guest room. Hardy was not questioning 'the help', not now, at any rate. He was standing by the far window looking down at the lights on the East River. A young uniformed cop was sitting in front of a stenotype machine waiting for whatever was to come next.

Hardy turned to us. He looked tired. "Nothing, I take it."

"That's how it is," Jerry said.

"I understand there's some coffee in the kitchen, Molloy," Hardy said to the cop. "Get yourself some. I'll call you when I need you."

"Bring you some, Lieutenant?"

"No, thanks. You guys?"

We didn't want coffee. The young patrolman took off.

"You're searching the hotel?" Hardy asked.

"Yes. It's a long, slow job unless we get lucky. And if we don't find him in some public place, then we're going to have to start waking up about seven hundred guests!"

"Chambrun wouldn't like that," Hardy said.

"Unfortunately he isn't here to object," Jerry said. "You have any luck with Battle's people?"

"It wouldn't seem so — on the surface," Hardy said. "Dr. Cobb was here in this room when the shot was fired. Battle went to bed early, as you know. Nine o'clock. Cobb came in here to snatch forty winks and get himself some oxygen."

"Oxygen?" I asked.

"Emphysema," Hardy said. He pointed to a brass cylinder that stood on the floor by the head of the bed. "He was pooped out from the trip and all the nonsense that went with it. He was breathing deeply when the shot was fired."

"He says," Jerry said.

Hardy nodded. "He says. He says he scrambled off the bed. That suggests speed, but with him I would think not.

He got out into the hallway just in time to see Butler, the bodyguard, come running out of the bathroom waving his gun. He thought for a moment Butler had done the shooting. He waddled into Battle's room and found him sitting up in bed, covers pulled up around him, in a state of shock. So much for Dr. Cobb."

"And the others?"

"Gaston, the chef, was in the kitchen

preparing a casserole of white fish in wine, Mr. Battle's favorite breakfast dish. He heard the shot. He didn't move at once because he thought it had come from somewhere out on the roof. Then he heard Butler shouting and he went along the hall to the bedroom. Allerton, the manservant, had taken the opportunity for a bath. He was soaking in a hot tub when he heard the shot. It took him a minute or two to get out, get dry, and into his bathrobe. He found everybody in the bedroom when he got there."

"None of them saw anyone in a stocking mask?"

"Gone," Hardy said. "Of course the key one is Butler, the bodyguard. He was sitting right outside the door of Battle's room, gun in his lap. I tried to get him to admit he'd fallen asleep. No dice. It would be better for him if he'd admit it, you understand. How did Stocking Face get past him if he was awake?"

"Easy," Jerry said. "It could have

been Allerton, or the chef, or Dr. Cobb coming from this end. They could go into the bathroom without passing Butler."

"Ten feet away with Butler having an unobstructed view? If Butler was awake, no one could have gotten into that room — except Butler."

"So it was Butler," Jerry said.

"Okay, then why isn't he taking the obvious out?" Hardy asked. "He should be saying: 'I goofed. It had been a long day. I fell asleep'. Instead he keeps insisting that he was awake and that no one could have gotten in the room without his seeing. I have to remind you that the windows are out. They're flush to the side of the building, barred, a big drop if the bars were faulty. Take a human fly."

"So none of it happened," Jerry said dryly.

"I haven't seen the bullet," Hardy said. "We've been kept out of the room since we got here."

"But I saw the bullet before you

were called," Jerry said. "It's there in the headboard. Naturally I left it for you to dig out."

"So it happened. So why doesn't Butler lie himself out of trouble instead of into it?"

"From what I've been hearing tonight, everything in this world is upside-down," I said.

Hardy looked at me. "What have you been hearing?"

"That nothing in Battle's world is ever what it seems to be," I said.

"Richard Cleaves?"

"Richard Cleaves and Peter Potter, who worked for Battle some time ago. What seems to be happening isn't happening."

"Potter hate him, too?" Hardy asked. I nodded.

Hardy sighed and stood up. "I guess I won't stand for any more delay," he said. "I'm going into that bedroom."

We followed him back to the living room. Kranepool was on the phone to his office. Dr. Cobb had leaned his head against the back of the couch. His bluish eyelids were closed. Hardy walked over to him. He touched the doctor's foot with his foot. The old man's eyes flew open.

"Oh, it's you, Lieutenant," he wheezed. He fumbled in the pocket of his robe for a cigarette.

"I'm going in, Doctor," Hardy said. "Want to stand by in case he comes to?"

"I have to protest," Cobb said. He struggled with his lighter and finally got his cigarette going.

"You go right ahead and protest, Doctor. You want to do it in writing, that would be fine with me. Keep you out of my hair." Hardy gestured to two plainclothes men who had been waiting in the corner of the room with cameras and other equipment. He started for the door to the bedroom.

That door opened before he reached it. George Battle, wearing a silk blue-and-white polka dot robe, stood there. I was surprised again by the extraordinary brightness of his blue eyes, the curious wreckage of what must have once been real male beauty. The eyes fastened on me.

"Where is Pierre?" he asked.

Behind me I heard Dr. Cobb whisper, "Christ, I gave him enough to knock him out for twelve hours!"

"Where's Allerton? I'd like some hot tea," Battle said.

He looked, I thought, like the disintegrated portrait of Dorian Grey. What had once been beauty of facial structure had become a kind of obscene caricature of what must have been a youthful elegance.

Allerton appeared from the kitchen as though he'd had some kind of advance notice, carrying a tray. On it was a teapot and two cups. He put the tray down on a side table and proceeded to pour tea into both cups. Battle's unnaturally bright eyes were fixed on him. Allerton picked up one of the cups and sipped from it. The king's taster! A sip evidently wasn't enough. Allerton looked apologetically at his employer and blew on the tea. Finally he was able to drink it. Only then did Battle step forward and pick up the second cup. His skin, very tight around his temples, seemed to glisten in the lamplight. He looked at Hardy.

"You are — ?"

"Lieutenant Hardy, Homicide, in charge of this case. I've been waiting to examine your room, Mr. Battle."

"So examine," Battle said, and sat down at the opposite end of the couch from Dr. Cobb, who kept looking at him with disbelief.

Hardy signaled to his technical crew and they all went into the bedroom. The bright blue eyes now shifted to Jerry Dodd and me.

"Where is Pierre?" Battle asked.

"He left when he understood the Doctor had put you to sleep," Jerry said.

Battle gave the doctor a contemptuous little smile. "Cobb and his magical herbs!" he said. "Tell Pierre I want him back here. I don't like the way things have been handled."

"I'm afraid I can't do that," Jerry said.

"Why not?"

"Because I don't know where he is," Jerry said. I saw that he was watching Battle closely. If there was anything to Cleaves' theory —

Kranepool joined us. "Somebody called Mr. Chambrun on the phone," he said, "pretending to be me. Mr. Chambrun started up here but he hasn't arrived. At the moment we don't know where he went."

"Who are you?" Battle asked.

"Lester Kranepool, assistant D.A., in charge."

"I thought that policeman was in charge," Battle said.

"For Homicide. I represent the District Attorney," Kranepool said.

"The usual inefficiency of a bureaucracy," Battle said. "Two men in charge." He pointed a long, thin finger at Kranepool. "You damn well better come up with results, young man. It's a miracle I wasn't killed here tonight. What are you doing to protect this penthouse now?"

"No one can get in here without an okay from us," Kranepool said.

"That's what they told me when I went to bed last night," Battle said. "How did that masked creature get in here?"

"We're not sure yet."

Battle glanced at his platinum wrist watch. His mouth curled down. "You've had over four hours. Would you or would you not call that incompetence?"

"We've been handicapped," Kranepool said, fighting outrage, "by not being able to talk to you."

"Why didn't you have Cobb wake me?"

"He said you were drugged out," Kranepool said.

"Faithful old Cobb," Battle said. He made it sound like an insult. "So your handicap is removed, Mr. Kranepool. Talk to me."

"I want a detailed account of everything that happened to you here tonight," Kranepool said.

Battle looked at him as if he smelled bad. "I told the whole thing to this man," and he jerked his head toward Jerry, "and to Pierre."

"Tell it to me," Kranepool said.

"My, my, authority does go to our head, doesn't it?" Battle said.

"Look, Mr. Battle, I don't give a damn how rich or important you are, I'm investigating a crime here. If you don't choose to cooperate, I'll have you taken downtown where you can think it over in a jail cell."

Battle actually smiled. "It would be almost worth while to let you try, Mr. Kranepool," he said. He turned to Jerry. "What are you doing to find Pierre?"

"What do you suggest, sir?" Jerry asked softly.

"A woman?" Battle asked.

"He was on his way here to help you," Jerry said. "Do you think he could be willingly sidetracked?"

Battle appeared to consider the possibility. "I suppose not," he said. "Not Pierre."

"Will you be good enough, Mr. Battle, to begin at the beginning," Kranepool said, his voice unsteady with anger.

"'In the beginning was the word'," Battle said. His paper-thin eyelids closed. "Shortly after nine o'clock I went to bed. I was exhausted. However, before I turned in, this man Dodd showed me exactly what precautions were being taken to protect me."

"You were expecting some sort of attack?" Kranepool asked.

Battle opened his eyes. "My dear young man, for the last thirty years I have expected an attack to be made on me, day and night. You are aware that I keep an armed bodyguard by my side, a doctor in case I should be wounded, a chef who prepares my meals, and a servant who tastes them before I do in case poison should be the method used. Do you think that's some kind of a parlor game?"

Kranepool restrained himself. "Dodd showed you what precautions had been taken," he said.

"He did. There were three hotel security men patrolling the roof outside. Dodd showed them to me. I saw them. There was an operator and a security man assigned to the elevator which comes to the roof. No one except the tenants of the other two penthouses could get up to this level."

"And no one did," Kranepool said.

"That is a reasonably comic remark, Mr. Kranepool," Battle said. "You should look at the bullet in the headboard of my bed. I don't propose to go on with this if you insist on nonsensical comments."

Kranepool was pale with anger, but he hung in there. "You were shown the sentries and the two men on the elevator," he said.

"I was shown them," Battle said, "but unfortunately I am not sufficiently psychic to have been aware of their inefficiency. Here, in this apartment, my man Butler was stationed outside my door. No one could come in without passing him. No one could come in by way of the bathroom, the door to which was in plain sight from where Butler was stationed."

"And he swears no one got past him or into the bathroom," Kranepool said.

"He is, of course, lying," Battle said. "He fell asleep."

"He says he didn't."

Battle smiled his feline smile. "Ask Dr. Cobb why he is lying."

Cobb cleared his throat, coughed, gasped for breath, and then said: "There are unpleasant punishments for inefficiency in this world," he said. "To have been asleep at his post could have most disastrous consequences for Butler."

"So you went to bed," Kranepool said.

"I went to my room. Allerton helped

me prepare for bed. I normally need some sort of medication — seconal or the like — to sleep for any length of time, but I was so thoroughly exhausted from the trip that I thought sleep would come without help. It was a very, very lucky decision on my part, because if I'd taken my sleeping pills, I would have been in the deepest part of my slumber when he came."

"The man in the stocking mask?"

"Who else, Mr. Kranepool? Are we, by chance, talking about someone else?"

"You slept," Kranepool said.

"Yes, but lightly; lightly enough, thank God, to have heard some slight movement he made — perhaps the squeak of a door, perhaps he collided with a chair or some other piece of furniture. I was suddenly wide awake, very aware that someone was in the room. I wasn't afraid at first. I thought it must be Allerton, or perhaps Dr. Cobb, checking to see if I was all right, if I needed something. I knew

Butler wouldn't have allowed anyone else into my quarters. I reached out and turned on the bedside lamp. I was frozen with terror when I saw him."

"You got a clear look at him?"

"A quick look, but very clear. He was standing just inside the bathroom door. He was wearing a pale brown stocking mask that covered his head — his hair, his face. He was pointing a gun at me. I find myself surprised now that I was able to move. My thought was to dive for the floor, and I projected myself toward the edge of the bed. We're talking about fractions of seconds, Mr. Kranepool, because as I moved he fired. The bullet struck the headboard, inches from me. I heard him cry out something — and as I turned my head, I saw him go out through the bathroom door. At the same moment Butler came bursting in through the main door there. I screamed at him and pointed to the bathroom."

"Just a minute," Kranepool said.

"You saw this man in the stocking mask go out through the bathroom?"

"Of course I saw him."

"And at the same instant Butler came through the other door?"

"I thought Butler could have seen him."

"Then Butler couldn't have been the man in the stocking mask, doubling back?"

"Nonsense," Battle said.

"Describe the gunman. Was he tall, short, fat, thin?"

"He could have been all of those things, my dear man. It was so quick. The mask was a light tan, with holes in it for his eyes. His clothes were dark, but don't ask me what they were — a suit, a sweater, a topcoat. I saw the mask, and I saw the gun aimed right between my eyes. Not much else registered."

"You say he cried out?"

"Yes. Something meaningless. He sounded surprised. And then he was gone."

"Do you know that Dodd, here, has a theory that the assassin was after Mr. Chambrun; that when he saw it was you, he jerked the gun away just in time?"

Battle looked at Jerry. "How very ingenious," he said.

"You don't believe it?"

"Of course I don't believe it. If he was after Pierre, wouldn't the sentries have made him wonder? Wouldn't the sleeping Butler have made him wonder? No, Pierre doesn't live under the threat of death that I do. He doesn't require guards. Anyone who knew him well enough — " Battle laughed — "well enough to want to kill him, would have known that something was out of key."

"Someone wanted him out of the way," Jerry said. "He hasn't disappeared by choice."

"My dear Dodd, of course someone wants him out of the way. Don't you know why?"

"Why?" Jerry said in a flat voice.

155

"Because there is just one man in the world I would trust to protect me beyond a shadow of a doubt. Pierre Chambrun doesn't make mistakes." His brow clouded. "Perhaps, like all of us, he is growing old. Because, if what you say is true, he has allowed himself to fall into a trap. God help me if I must count on you people and the police to protect me. I came here because I could count on Pierre. Who can I depend on now?"

I could have sworn he wasn't afraid; he was more like some kind of game-player, delighted with a puzzle.

Hardy came out of the bedroom, and with him was Butler, the bodyguard. Battle raised what must have been a cup of cold tea to his lips, his eyes bright over the rim.

"Show me exactly where you were sitting," Hardy said to Butler.

If anyone was afraid in the room it was Butler, the tough guy, the gunslinger. Little beads of sweat stood out on his forehead. He glanced at

Battle as if he was pleading for some kind of cue from his employer. Battle's eyes were laughing at him.

"I had that chair there, back to the door," Butler said. He moved a Windsor armchair into place. Hardy closed the door to the bedroom. "From there I could see the front door and the doors to the bedrooms and the bathrooms down the hall."

"You sat in the chair," Hardy said.

"I sat in the chair, Lieutenant. I had taken off my shoulder holster and it was resting in my lap with my gun in it. I had a magazine." He looked around and saw a copy of *Time* on the end table. "That's it. Somebody must have moved it when they all came in here."

"'They all'?" Hardy asked.

"Dr Cobb, Gaston, Allerton. Then one of the sentries from the roof. The sentry phoned downstairs, and Dodd and Mr. Chambrun came."

"Let's not move quite so fast," Hardy said. "You set the chair in place, you sat in it with your gun in your lap, and you read a magazine."

"And you fell asleep," Battle said in a faraway voice.

A little trickle of sweat ran down Butler's cheek. He moistened his lips. He focused on Battle. I could sense the question he was asking: "Is that what you want me to say?" There was no indication from Battle.

"I did not fall asleep," Butler said, his voice shaken.

Hardy sat down in the chair. "So you were here." He turned his head from side to side. "You're right. No one could have approached the bedroom or the bathroom doors without your seeing them. And you insist no one did?"

"I didn't see anyone," Butler said.

"That's not quite the same as saying no one did."

"All right then, no one did!"

"And yet someone was in the room and did shoot at Mr. Battle," Hardy said. "How do you account for that?"

"There is only one way to account for it," Butler said. "The man was already in the room when I took my position here outside the door."

"My dear Edward," Battle said, "you searched the apartment when we first arrived. You said it was all clear."

Butler lowered his head. "I must have overlooked someplace he could have been hiding."

"How careless," Battle said. "Almost criminally careless, wouldn't you say, Edward?"

Butler looked as though he was going to cry.

Hardy stood up and pushed the chair aside. "Let's see what places you could have overlooked," he said.

Jerry and I crowded after them into the doorway, with Kranepool pushing past us to be in on it. One of the plainclothes men already in the room was dusting for fingerprints. The other was kneeling by the big queen-sized bed taking pictures of the headboard. He stood up and took a piece of folded tissue out of his pocket.

"Here's the bullet, Lieutenant. Slug from a thirty-eight police special, like Dodd thought it was. Trajectory places the fire place from somewhere near the bathroom door, which is the way Battle described it."

Hardy nodded. "Get it to ballistics," he said. He looked around the room. "How about the clothes closet?" he asked Butler.

"I went through it. Mr. Chambrun had removed his own clothes. It was bare — just hangers — ready for Mr. Battle. No place for anyone to hide."

Hardy, unperturbed, walked over to the barred windows. There were two sets of heavy drapes on either side. "How about here?"

"I looked behind them," Butler said. "I pushed and poked at them. So help me God, there was no one in this room."

"You couldn't hide under that box-spring bed," Hardy said, sounding almost cheerful. "How about the bathroom?"

"There's no place there, Lieutenant. I looked in the shower. There's a medicine cabinet. No place."

Hardy had moved to the bathroom door. "How about this laundry hamper?" he asked.

"For Christ sake, Lieutenant, nobody could fit into that."

"You didn't look in it?"

"Why should I?"

Hardy nodded and came back into the bedroom. "You're right," he said. "A man couldn't hide there." He looked at Butler, shaking his head slowly. "You tell an interesting story, Mr. Butler. No one was hidden in the room, no one could have come into it without your seeing him. Since you didn't see anyone there was, by your story, no one here. And yet there is a bullet in the headboard and Mr. Battle saw his attacker go out through the bathroom."

"I didn't say no one could have come

out through the bathroom without my seeing him," Butler said. He sounded desperate. "The minute I heard the shot I — "

"You admit you heard the shot?"

"Sure I heard it. I never said there was no shot."

"That's so, you didn't."

"The minute I heard the shot I jumped out of the chair, pushed it aside and came in here. Mr. Battle was sitting up in bed, covers pulled up around him. He waved and pointed at the bathroom. I ran into the bathroom and out into the hall. The man could have escaped that way without being seen. Cobb was in his room, Allerton in his, Gaston in the kitchen. He could have gotten away without being seen."

"But since he never got in?" Hardy asked gently.

"If I knew the answer to that, I'd feel an effing lot better."

"How's that?"

"'Effing' is Edward's way of cleaning

up an old Anglo-Saxon word," Battle said from the doorway. "Listen, Edward, I promise not to boil you in oil if you will admit that you fell asleep at your post. Human weakness is human weakness."

"So help me, Mr. Battle, I — "

"So have it your way, Edward," Battle said.

"I've had just about enough of this double-talk," Jerry Dodd said. "I've got a man to find. Let's go, Mark."

A telephone in the living room rang. It was the outside line. There's a difference between the outside ring and the sound you get from a switchboard call. Jerry, who had been moving out, got to it first. I heard his sharp "Yes?" I knew he was hoping it might be some word about Chambrun. He turned away from the phone.

"It's for Mr. Battle," he said.

Battle waved a 'no' at him and went back to the couch.

"Mr. Battle isn't able to come to

the phone just now," Jerry said. Then I saw him tense. "Say that again." He covered the mouthpiece with his hand and his eyes, bright as two newly minted dimes, were fixed on Battle. "I quote," he said. "If you want to see your friend Chambrun alive again, you'd better come to the phone."

Battle, looking shocked, stood up and walked across the room, where he took the phone from Jerry. Jerry, muttering under his breath, raced for the bedroom where there was an extension to this outside line.

"George Battle here," Battle said. "Yes — yes — yes, I understand. There's no way to get that kind of money in cash until after the banks open in the morning. Yes, I'm listening." The listening occupied a full minute. Then Battle said: "It's perfectly clear. How do I know that Chambrun is safe? — Trust you, you swine, why should I trust you? — Yes, we'll wait for your call." Battle put down the phone slowly.

Jerry came charging in from the bedroom.

"No time to trace the call," he said. He looked around at us. "It would seem the boss has been kidnaped. They're demanding a hundred grand in ransom money. They'll call tomorrow morning — this morning — when we've had a chance to raise the cash in unmarked tens and twenties." He looked at me. "You, Mark, are to be ready to deliver the money."

Battle was still standing by the phone, his face looking like a wax mask. "I will, of course, arrange for the money," he said.

"Where am I supposed to take the money?" I asked.

"They'll let us know in the morning."

"You ought to notify the FBI," Hardy said.

"No!" Battle said sharply. "The money is meaningless. I want Pierre safe. They warned me specifically!"

"They always do," Hardy said, "and the people who listen let them get away with their crime."

"You risk Pierre's safety, Lieutenant, and I'll have you served up for dinner with an apple in your mouth!" Battle said.

3

MY legs felt rubbery under me as I walked along the second-floor corridor toward Chambrun's office. I think, when Chambrun first turned up missing, that I had subconsciously refused to believe that he was in any real danger. For some reason that would be easily explained he had taken off without telling us where he was going or why. The phone call to George Battle had put an end to that little bit of hopeful rationalizing. Chambrun had disappeared against his will, was being held against his will, and God alone knew whether he would be returned to us unhurt and all in one piece.

Jerry Dodd was not someone who would leave any manholes uncovered. I had supposed he would call off the search for Chambrun in the hotel.

Instead he gave strict instructions that no word about the kidnaping should leak and the search should go on. His thinking was pretty grim.

"They'd make a try for the money whether the boss is safe or not," he said. "Knowing him, they may never have gotten him out of the hotel. He could very well have put up a fight and been clobbered. We'll keep searching for him here until we know for certain he hasn't been dumped somewhere, dead or dying."

It was left for me to tell Betsy Ruysdale what we knew. She would have to be told.

Ruysdale and Shelda were still in Ruysdale's office when I got there. It looked as if they'd been keeping alive on coffee and cigarettes. Ruysdale stood up as I came in, and I suspect she sensed that I had some kind of bad news.

"We've had a call," I told her. "The boss has been kidnaped. They're asking for a hundred thousand dollars' ransom. When we have the money in the morning, we'll get instructions on where to deliver it. It seems I'm to be the messenger boy."

"Why you, Mark?" Shelda asked. She was afraid for me, which didn't make me unhappy.

"The answer to that is fairly simple," Ruysdale said. "They evidently know that Mark will follow instructions to the letter. They'd choose someone they know loves Mr. Chambrun and can be counted on to do nothing that would risk his safety." She turned toward the telephones on her desk. "We've got to find a way to raise the money," she said. "George Kobler isn't going to relish being waked up at three in the morning, but — "

"Battle has already agreed to put up the money," I said. "The phone call was made to him."

"I thought the doctor had put him to sleep?"

"Whatever Cobb gave him didn't hold him for long," I said. "He's

169

bright as a button and full of double talk, insults, and snide side attacks. He's a character. How the people who work for him put up with him I'll never know."

"They understand him," Shelda said.

She'd been working for him for a year, I remembered. "Does he throw curves at you?" I asked.

"He has almost no social life," Shelda said. "No parties or casual guests. The only people he can play games with are the members of his household — Ed Butler, Dr. Cobb, Allerton, Gaston, me and Gloria, the other secretary."

"Where is Gloria, by the way?"

"Vacation," Shelda said. "He didn't feel he needed her on this trip. She stayed in Cannes. He's pretty cruel with his wisecracks a lot of the time, but when it comes to any kind of real problem, some kind of trouble you might be in, he's kind and generous to a fault. You don't think people like Ed Butler, and Dr. Cobb, and Allerton and Gaston would stand by him if they didn't know that, do you? They've all been with him a long time. They wouldn't put up with him if they didn't understand him, would they?"

"You didn't find him hard to take?" I asked.

She shook her head slowly. "He's not like anyone you've ever met," she said. "Eccentric, a hypochondriac, in constant fear of some kind of physical attack. And yet — well, I don't quite know how to put it. I've never known anyone so intensely alive in terms of his interests, unless it's Mr. Chambrun."

"You're saying they're alike?" Ruysdale asked.

"Not at all. But Mr. Chambrun spends every waking hour concerned with the Beaumont and its operation." I thought I detected a faint little smile at the corners of Ruysdale's mouth, as if she was thinking that she knew of times when that wasn't so. "Mr. Battle has interests all over the world. He has a dozen clocks in his study in Cannes that tell him what time it is in London, New York, Moscow, Tokyo, other places. At first I didn't know what he had a secretary to do. He handles everything by telephone. There is almost no correspondence, in or out. He seems to keep everything in his head. During the day he will call me to take notes every half hour or so. The same thing at night. I've never known him to sleep more than forty-five minutes at a stretch. He dictates to me, stuff about the stock markets, the price of commodities, the price of money, the production of oil wells, of mines; stuff about men in politics and in industry, about combines and mergers, about diplomatic deals and alliances and treaties. Most of it means nothing to me. I transcribe my shorthand and type up the notes, and I swear he never looks at them. There are tons of them filed away, unread, unreferred to. He's never asked me to dig one of them out for him. It's as if once he'd put his ideas into words they were stored away in a computer bank inside his head. He's never asked me for a name, or a telephone number, or an address. They're all in his head."

"No small talk?"

"Only what you call his snide little side attacks," Shelda said. "He teases Dr. Cobb about his appetite, his overindulgence in alcohol, his chain smoking when he's seriously ill with emphysema. Gaston is an obvious homo, and Mr. Battle teases him about imaginary male lovers. Allerton, poor guy, gets quite the worst of it. He'll be asked about the right fork to use at dinner, constantly kidded about etiquette, and the middle-class cockney family he came from, and how on earth did he come by his elegant manners. He's teased about his job of tasting Mr. Battle's food, warned that he may drop dead after a mouthful of it, forced to do nasty little clean-up jobs. But I suspect Allerton will be a rich man when the time comes for him to retire. Butler appears to be such a tough guy, but Mr. Battle manages to whittle him down. Sometimes I think Butler is afraid of him, that maybe Mr. Battle has something on him."

"And how did he tease you?" I asked.

A faint color rose in Shelda's cheeks. "He seemed to know about you and me, Mark. He kept asking me if I was saving myself for you — when I had evenings off. If I was, I was wasting my youth."

"And were you?" I asked.

"We will talk about that some other time," she said.

Ruysdale broke that up. "It's going on four o'clock," she said. "You'll be needed, Mark, shortly after nine o'clock when the banks have opened. God knows how far you'll have to go with the money or what it's going to involve. You've got time for five hours to get some sleep." She glanced at Shelda. "And I mean sleep."

★ ★ ★

If you had asked me if I would sleep, I'd have expressed doubt. I had wanted time with Shelda. My deep concern for Chambrun was gnawing at my gut. I went to my room, left a call at the switchboard for eight o'clock, and went out like a fuse-blown light. My bedside telephone must have rung for a solid minute before I managed to reach out for it and thank the operator for calling me.

It was pouring rain outside. I shaved, showered, and dressed while the percolator in my kitchenette bubbled away. At the last minute I had coffee, toast, and a slice of cold ham for breakfast. I hadn't had enough sleep and I felt uptight. In the next hour I'd know what my assignment was going to be, and how I carried it out might determine whether or not we got Chambrun back safe. It was a scary thought.

I guess I had no complaints, because nobody else had had much or any sleep. I went down to the lobby, carrying a raincoat and hat, to get the special elevator to the roof. On the surface everything looked normal. I called the penthouse on a house phone and was instructed to come up at once. The lobby clock showed a quarter to nine.

Upstairs things did not look as unruffled as the lobby. Battle and his staff were not in evidence in the living room, but Jerry was there, needing a shave, eyes red-rimmed with fatigue. They had, he told me, continued the search of the hotel all night. Unless Chambrun was being held in one of the occupied rooms in the hotel, he wasn't on the premises.

"That's a good sign, isn't it?" I asked. "It means he wasn't slugged right on the spot — the minute he stepped out of his office."

"We hope!"

"Anything new here?"

Jerry laughed and glanced at Hardy, who was sitting in a corner of the couch frowning at his notebook. "The police department discovered a new dish for breakfast. White fish cooked in wine."

Hardy looked up at me and grinned. "The cook has taken a shine to me," he said. He closed the notebook and put it in his pocket. "The Master is having his in the bedroom at this moment. It is very good with little new potatoes covered with butter and parsley sauce. If you care for gooseberry preserve on toast, with sweet butter, it adds. And the coffee would put Chambrun to shame."

"It is hoped the special breakfast will sharpen his brain," Jerry said.

Hardy glanced at his watch. "Going on nine," he said. "The money should get here from the bank in about twenty-five minutes. You want advice?"

"Sure."

"Do whatever you're told, Mark." He'd turned serious. "Don't make demands. If they don't turn Chambrun over to you, don't argue. Give them the money." He glanced at the bedroom door. "That old buzzard can be bled for a lot more than a hundred grand.

They may try it. Don't try to be a hero. You understand, it's idiotic not to have called the FBI, but you can't find too many friends who can dish out this kind of bread without wincing."

"Have you made any progress?" I asked.

"I kept hoping you wouldn't ask," Hardy said. "On what we've got, it seems almost impossible this masked gunman could have come from the outside. So you pays your money and you takes your choice — Butler, Allerton, Dr. Cobb, or my whitefish cooker."

"And you're letting them run around loose?"

"I've got a man in there," Hardy said. "Under protest, would you believe? He's watching Gaston bring in the breakfast, Allerton taste and serve it, Butler acting like a watchdog, with Dr. Cobb standing by in case he needs an Alka-Seltzer. You know why I let that happen?"

"Tell me," I said.

178

"I tell our friend Battle that I'm convinced no one got in or out of the penthouse. That means that Stocking Mask was one of his people. I suggest they be removed and we get some other people to take care of him. He laughed in my face. He told me I was some kind of mental defective. These, he told me, are trusted people, been with him for years. He would trust them sooner than he would his own mother. I will let them alone or he will bring pressure to bear — maybe even from the White House, if necessary. I think the would-be murderer is right here in the apartment and all I can do about it is check, and re-check, and wait for something to happen."

"If the man who fired the shot is here, then the gun he used must be here," I said.

"I have searched every room, every drawer, every cupboard, and those four guys down to their skins. No gun. Don't tell me it could have been thrown out a window or down the garbage disposal chute. It's not on the roof; it didn't reach the sidewalk or any overhang; we've sifted every bit of garbage and trash at the bottom of the garbage chute. It's been a long night, friend."

"If you think it's been long for you, Mr. Hardy," Battle said from the doorway, "you can imagine how long it's been for me, knowing that a killer can come and go without your knowing how." He had a way of appearing in the middle of conversations. He was wearing dark trousers, a red velvet smoking jacket, a white ascot. He looked unnaturally cheerful for a man whose life was on the line. He glanced at his wrist watch. "The money should be here from the bank presently. Have you made any preparations to trace their phone call when it comes, Dodd?"

"Of course," Jerry said.

"Cancel them," Battle said. "If there's any clicking on the line, they'll know. I won't have Pierre placed in any unnecessary danger."

"Suppose Mark hands them the money and they just walk off with it and Mr. Chambrun isn't returned? We don't have any kind of lead!" Jerry said.

"The call will almost certainly be made from a coin box," Hardy said. "Tracing it isn't going to do much good, Jerry."

"At last you show some signs of common sense, Lieutenant," Battle said.

"We aim to please," Hardy said, undisturbed. "Unfortunately it doesn't please you to be told that one of the four men on your staff tried to kill you last night. All I can do is sit here and make certain that he doesn't try again — at least until the Commissioner decides I'm wrong and that I'm not earning my money sitting around here eating gourmet breakfasts."

Battle's eyes narrowed. "I may have to ask the Commissioner to assign someone to the job whose thinking is a little more flexible than yours."

The house phone rang and Jerry got to it ahead of Allerton, who came out of the bedroom. "Dodd here." I realized the call from the kidnapers wouldn't come on the house phone. "Send them up," Jerry said. He put down the phone and turned back to us. "It's the messenger from the bank and a couple of guards."

The room was suddenly crowded. Battle's people appeared, as though the telephone ring had been a signal. With them were two of Hardy's men. Battle had appropriated one end of the couch and seemed to be enjoying the moment. A very shaky Dr. Cobb asked me for a light for his cigarette. His lighter had run out of juice.

"Remarkable man, your Mr. Battle," I said, as I held a light for him. The room was suddenly loud with talk, so what we said was between us.

Cobb nodded, his cigarette bobbing up and down in my lighter flame.

"You knock him out for twelve hours,

he sleeps a couple, and now he looks brighter than any of us."

Cobb drew a deep, wheezing breath. "When there's genuine activity, he can outlast anyone you care to name," he said. His watery eyes fixed on me. "You nervous?"

"Would you expect something else?"

"Not really. Your detective friend's solved the case, you know. It's me, or Edward, or Allerton, or Gaston."

"You've got an easy out," I said.

"Oh?" His eyebrows shot up.

"Explain how Stocking Mask got in and out and you're home free."

He gave me his flabby-lipped smile. "Just before they strap me in the electric chair, Mr. Haskell, I'll do that."

"They've done away with the electric chair," I said.

"Then just before the dungeon door closes on me — "

"You mean you know?" I thought, of course, he was kidding.

He laughed, and the laughter developed into a coughing fit. "Of course I know," he finally managed to gasp. "Don't you, Haskell?"

The doorbell rang, and Jerry Dodd went to answer it. We were all watching. I felt a tug at my sleeve. It was Cobb, looking as if he was about to strangle. "What I said is privileged, Haskell. Just our little joke. Right?"

I wasn't in the mood for jokes, macabre or otherwise. The bank messenger was a little man in a dark suit who looked like an undertaker's assistant. He was surrounded by two uniformed bank guards and two uniformed patrolmen. He was carrying a square black attaché case that presumably contained a hundred thousand dollars in unmarked tens and twenties. He took the case over to the couch and handed it to Battle.

"Will you be good enough to sign a receipt for this, sir?" he asked.

"Without counting it?" Battle asked.

"It was counted in front of Mr. Colchester, the bank president, and Mr.

Worthington, the first vice-president, sir."

"But can they count?" Battle asked. He was enjoying himself, and I was getting sick of his needle.

"Well, sir," the unhappy messenger said, "I'd be glad to count it in your presence."

"You do just that," Battle said.

The little man put the case down on the couch beside Battle and opened it. A small crowd collected around him. I don't suppose any of us had seen that much money in cash before. He began to count.

The outside phone rang. Jerry Dodd grabbed it up, and the room was suddenly dead still except for the messenger's whispered counting.

Jerry turned to me. "For you, Mark," he said. His hand covered the mouthpiece. "This is it, baby. Play it cool."

My legs had to be forced to work. The minute I took the phone from him Jerry raced for the bedroom and the extension there.

"Mark Haskell here," I said.

A thick, muffled voice came over the line. It sounded as though the man was talking through a towel or a handkerchief. "It's not going to do any good for anyone to listen in, Haskell."

"What do you want me to do?"

"You are to bring the money to 134 East 65th Street," the voice said. "You will carry it up to the second floor where someone will take it from you. You've got that?"

"Yes."

"Now, listen very carefully, Haskell. You will be watched from the minute you step off the elevator into the hotel lobby, every step of the way to the address I've given you. If you are followed, there won't be anyone to accept the money. If police appear at that address, there won't be anyone. And if there is no one there, you can save the money for an elaborate funeral. Is that clear?"

"Yes."

"It's only about three blocks from where you are now, Haskell. If you walk briskly, you should make it in about twelve minutes. If you haven't arrived in fifteen minutes, there won't be anyone there and you can start notifying the mourners."

There was a click off and he was gone.

Jerry came running out of the bedroom. He pushed the messenger aside and snapped the case closed. "No time to count or talk," he said. "I'll go down in the elevator with you."

I grabbed up my raincoat and hat and took the bag from him. It was heavier than I'd expected. The elevator was at the roof level. We stepped in with the operator and a plainclothes man who was assigned to the car.

"They're not stupid," Jerry said. "They've made the pickup close by and set a time limit for you. There's no time for us to get clever. The minute you step off the elevator, you'll be watched. So walk straight to where you're going, baby, and walk fast!"

I nodded. My mouth felt dry.

"He's right. You should make it in twelve minutes. Now, listen to me, Mark. Give him the money. Don't talk or argue or make demands to see Chambrun safe. Just give it to him."

"Yes."

"Then get to a phone as quickly as you can and ring me here. If we haven't heard from you in twenty-five minutes, we'll come looking for you."

"That could screw it up, couldn't it?"

"They'll be long gone then."

The elevator reached the lobby level and the doors opened. Jerry didn't move. I looked at him. I didn't want to leave him.

"Go!" he said. "If I show, they may think I'm trying to spot them."

I stepped out into the busy lobby and the elevator doors closed behind me. I was on my own.

I carried the black case under my arm, holding onto it for dear life. I crossed the lobby without looking right or left and went through the revolving door to the side street and into the sluicing rain. Jesus, I don't think I ever felt so alone in my whole life.

I guess there were people on the streets, but I didn't see them. I had the bag under my arm, and I was almost jogging, and the rain was beating against my face so that I kept my hat pulled down and my head lowered. It must have taken five minutes or more to come down from the penthouse to the lobby and out onto the street. I didn't have much time to cover the one long block east, the two blocks north, and half a block east again. I didn't wait for the traffic lights to turn my way at the corners, and once I heard someone yelling at me and realized I'd been almost run down by a taxi. When I stopped outside the address of 65th Street, I glanced at my watch. The whole trip, from penthouse to there, had taken me exactly thirteen minutes.

It was an old brownstone house, looking pretty shabby. I saw a ROOM FOR RENT sign in one of the downstairs windows. I had just two minutes to get to the second floor, and I felt panicked. Suppose I couldn't get in? Suppose I had to wait for someone to answer a ring of the doorbell?

I tried the front door and it was unlocked. I stumbled into a dark foyer and saw a dirty stairway leading up into gloom. I took it, two steps at a time, and reached the second floor with a minute to spare. I stood there, breathing hard, clinging to the black bag full of money, waiting for something to happen.

A door at the end of the hall opened. A man came out and closed the door behind him. Like me, he was wearing a raincoat and a soft hat with the brim pulled down. I prayed he would turn out to be my contact. When he was only a few feet from me, I knew he was.

He was wearing a pale, brown stocking mask. He looked like something out of a 1930's horror movie, faceless with two little peepholes for eyes. He came straight up to me and held out his left hand, gesturing toward the bag.

"Where is Mr. Chambrun?" I asked him.

He repeated the gesture toward the bag, this time with impatience. Jerry had told me not to ask him anything, not to argue with him, just to give him the money. But, somehow, I had to try.

"Please tell me where he is," I said.

He took a step closer to me, raised his right hand, and brought it down in a chopping movement to the side of my neck. I don't remember falling.

★ ★ ★

When I opened my eyes, I found myself looking up into Jerry Dodd's anxious face. It flashed through my mind that I must have been lying there

191

a good twenty minutes. He couldn't have gotten here any sooner than that. I tried to turn my head and I thought my neck was broken.

"Easy," Jerry said. He put his arm under my shoulders and helped me to sit up. "Looks like you met up with a karate expert."

"The money?" I asked. I found I had the voice of a severe laryngitis victim.

"He got it. Did you see him?"

"Stocking mask," I said.

Jerry made a whistling sound between his teeth. "Let me help you stand up," he said.

I managed, somehow, with the dark hallway spinning around me for a few seconds. I ached all over. I must have hit the floor hard when I was struck. But the dizziness began to subside.

"Can you describe him?" Jerry asked.

"Raincoat, hat, and that damned stocking mask. He looked like Vincent Price in *The Invisible Man*."

"Tall like that?"

"Nearer my height," I said.

"Was he waiting here for you?"

I shook my head and wished I hadn't. "He came out of that room there at the end of the hall. The minute I hit this landing here, he came out. I — I made a mistake. I asked him where the boss was, and he chopped me down."

A little muscle rippled along the line of Jerry's jaw. He felt in the pocket of his raincoat and produced a small handgun. "Let's have a look," he said.

We walked down the hall to the door of the room. Jerry hesitated, and then, with his left hand, he tried turning the doorknob, his gun at the ready. The door made a faint squeaking sound as it opened, and Jerry stepped quickly into the room.

It was a dismal, dirty little place. There was a bed, a bureau, and a straight-backed chair. Sitting in the chair was a man with a piece of wide adhesive taped over his mouth, his arms locked behind the chair.

It was Chambrun.

★ ★ ★

Chambrun's eyes were two bright, glittering slits in their deep pouches. Jerry stood in front of him.

"This is going to hurt," he said.

He got his fingernails under one edge of the adhesive tape and gave it a quick, sharp tug. Chambrun swore softly under his breath. He moved his mouth to try to get some feeling back into it. I had gone around behind the chair and saw that his wrists were handcuffed together.

"We're going to need some kind of a steel saw to get these things off," I said.

"The keys are on the bureau," Chambrun said.

We had him free in a matter of seconds. He stood up and stretched painfully. "Remind me," he said, "to consider permanent retirement. I let that sonofabitch take me like Grant took Richmond. Walked right into it. What's happened at the hotel?"

194

"You happened," Jerry said. "We've been searching the place all night for you."

"How did you happen to find me here — for which I'm grateful?"

"Mark was ordered to bring the money here."

"Money?"

"Ransom money, boss. A hundred G's he got away with."

"Where in God's name did you get that kind of money? Wait. Don't tell me. George Battle put it up?"

"Right," Jerry said. "Listen, boss, did you ever get a look at this man?"

Chambrun was flexing his fingers and then rubbing his bruised wrists. "I walked out of my office thinking I'd had a call from Kranepool to come up to the penthouse. Ruysdale took the call. She didn't know Kranepool's voice, of course, and had no reason to doubt it was him. This creep in the stocking mask was waiting right outside the office and stuck a gun at my throat. I was to get us out of the hotel without being seen if I wanted to keep my head on. I wanted to keep my head on, so I showed him a way out through the basement. We walked here, would you believe it, gun in my back. Three blocks. Would you believe we never saw a cop, never passed close enough to anyone for me to try anything? I was brought up here, handcuffed to that chair, my mouth taped. I never saw him again until about an hour ago. I was able to make some banging noises with my feet on the floor. No one ever responded. God, I need a shave and a hot shower and some clean clothes. We can talk on the way."

"You and Mark go," Jerry said. "I'm going to find the superintendent or the landlady of this joint and do a little arm twisting. Tell Art Stein at the hotel that the ball game is over and we won."

"You're dreaming," Chambrun said. "We've lost every step of the way so far. Let's go, Mark." I turned my head and I guess he saw me wince. "What happened to you?"

"Your friend gave him a very expert karate chop," Jerry said.

"So we have two scores to settle," Chambrun said.

We went down and out onto the street. I looked around for a cab, but Chambrun wanted to walk. "Got to get my circulation going again — if you can stand it, Mark."

So we walked. The rain had let up and was not much more than a gentle drizzle. I offered Chambrun my raincoat, but he said at least one of us might as well be dry when we got home. On the way I brought him up to date; chiefly Hardy's theory that Stocking Mask was one of Battle's people.

"But that's blown sky high, unless there are a lot of people running around in masks," I said. "The man who came out of your room and slugged me couldn't have been any of Mr. Battle's crew. They're all back in the penthouse, being watched over by Hardy." Then I remembered something. "How well do you know Dr. Cobb?"

"Known him casually for twenty years — about the time he's worked for George. Why?"

"Maybe he was kidding," I said, "but he told me he knows how the masked man got into the penthouse. Afterwards he urged me not to tell anyone what he'd said. I couldn't push him about it because just then the phone call came from the guy who had you with instructions on how to deliver the money. I suspect Cobb likes a joke, but somehow this didn't sound like a joke."

"There's very little that's a joke in George Battle's world," Chambrun said. "Does Ruysdale know — about me, I mean?"

"She was there almost the minute it happened. Naturally, she's worried sick. But you better look out. She knows as much about running the Beaumont as you do."

He seemed to suppress a smile. "All the people I train know their jobs," he said. He turned west a block too soon. "I want to take you in the cellar way — the way I was taken out. I don't want to be seen until I'm cleaned up."

I've been working at the Beaumont for some years, but there's always something new about it. I guess I knew, without having seen them, that there were ways to get trash up from the basement to the street level where it could be picked up by the Sanitation Department. There were two big iron doors, level with the sidewalk. Chambrun pressed a button and stood back, and presently the doors were lifted by an elevator which came right up onto the street. We stepped on the elevator and went down, the iron doors closing over our heads. Chambrun found a light switch in the dark and we walked along a narrow passage to where the regular banks of elevators were located.

"My friend and I came down from the second floor, and I showed him how to get out because I didn't feel I wanted to risk his getting nervous."

Chambrun rang for an elevator and it came down, manned by an operator.

"Gee, Mr. Chambrun," the man said, "they been looking all over hell for you."

"I took a night off," Chambrun said. "Second floor, please, Paul." He knows everybody's names, first and last, in a staff of over seven hundred people.

We got off at two and walked down the hall to his office. Miss Ruysdale was in the outer room. She got up from her desk more quickly than I'd ever seen her move.

"Good morning, Ruysdale," Chambrun said, completely casual. He kept right on walking toward his office.

"Good morning, Mr. Chambrun," she said. She looked as if someone had turned on a light inside her. "May I let the staff know that you're back?"

He turned at the door and smiled for the first time since we'd found him. "If you think it will spread joy," he said. "Thanks, Ruysdale, for holding the fort."

"Thanks for getting back," she said.

Chambrun has a dressing room with a couch in it for occasional catnaps, also shaving equipment and changes of clothes. While he disappeared to freshen up, Ruysdale began reporting to an anxious staff and I called Lieutenant Hardy in the penthouse.

"Not hurt?" Hardy asked, when I'd reported.

"Maybe his feelings," I said. "The important thing, Lieutenant, is that the man who held him and who slugged me was wearing a stocking mask. It couldn't have been one of your four suspects unless one of them got away from you both last night and this morning."

"Damn!" Hardy said. I heard a long sigh. "Sounds like we have to start over."

"Where?"

"Who knows?" Hardy said. "I'd still stake my job on the fact that no one could have gotten in here from the outside to take a shot at Battle." He sighed again. "Tell your boss I'm glad he's back. Maybe he knows something I don't know."

I stopped Ruysdale long enough to ask her where Shelda had gone.

"Up to the penthouse," she told me. "She is Mr. Battle's secretary, you know."

"It'll take the boss fifteen minutes to get cleaned up," I said. "Any reason I shouldn't run up there to see her? She's naturally worried about me. And the boss, too, of course."

"I'll tell him where you are," Ruysdale said.

There was no way on earth I could have known that my decision to go up to the penthouse at that moment was actually going to save Shelda's life.

★ ★ ★

Things seemed to be at a low level of action in the penthouse when

I was finally taken up there with Hardy's permission acquired. Hardy and Kranepool were in the living room, but there was no sign of Battle or any of the others with the exception of Allerton. This impeccable manservant had set up a coffee percolator on a corner table along with a platter of cold meats and hard rolls. He appeared when I was admitted and, without asking, brought me a cup of coffee and a plate of food. I was grateful. The coffee at least was a lifesaver.

"Miss Mason is here, isn't she, Allerton?" I asked.

"Yes, sir. She's in Mr. George's quarters. Would you like to see her?"

"Very much," I said.

"I'll see if she can be spared, sir," Allerton said. He went over to the bedroom door and knocked softly. The door was opened by Butler, and Allerton was allowed to go in.

Kranepool and Hardy wanted details of my trip with the money, and I had to tell it all over again. Naturally they had endless questions about the man in the stocking mask — his height, his weight, anything I'd noticed about his raincoat and hat that might be distinctive. Hardy wondered if, perhaps, there had been a missing button, or a tear in the material. The sound of his voice?

"He never spoke," I told them. "He just came toward me, holding out his left hand, and when I asked him where Mr. Chambrun was, he chopped me down. I should think Mr. Chambrun could tell you a lot more than I can. I don't suppose the thing with me lasted more than thirty seconds."

"I'll go down to see Chambrun," Kranepool said, and started for the door.

"Give him a few minutes," I said. "He had a tough night. My guess is he'll be up here in a few minutes when he's cleaned up."

And then Shelda came out of the Great Man's bedroom and I wasn't very interested in Kranepool's problems anymore. One look at her and I knew she'd worried about me and that she was glad to see me still in one piece. The hell with Kranepool and Hardy, I thought, and I went over to her and kissed her, and then led her over to a far corner of the room. She was hanging onto my arm and I could feel that she was trembling.

"You're all right?" she asked.

"Best I've felt since a year ago when you went away."

Her eyes were such a warm, deep blue. All of her was so inviting, so precious.

"Mr. Chambrun?"

"Not hurt," I said, "except maybe his feelings. What's with G. Battle?"

"Anxious to see Mr. Chambrun. Mr. Chambrun is the only person he really trusts."

"I love you," I said.

"Mark — darling!"

I kissed her again. I could hear Kranepool on the phone to Miss Ruysdale, asking her to get Chambrun up here as fast as she could.

"When this is cleaned up, we'll go somewhere," I said to Shelda. "Way to-hell-and-gone somewhere."

"Yes," she said.

The front doorbell rang, an irregular ring that was obviously some kind of signal. Hardy answered it. It was his man stationed on the elevator. He had half a dozen letters in his hand.

"Mail for Mr. Battle," he said.

Hardy took it and the man went out again to his post. Hardy shuffled through the letters, disinterested. "I suppose you better take these in to him," he said to Shelda.

She sighed and went toward him. At the same moment Allerton came out of the bedroom and saw what was happening. He gave me the tiniest little smile.

"I'll take them in," he said.

"Thanks ever so much," Shelda said.

Allerton took the letters and went back into the bedroom.

It's funny, but I can't remember what Shelda and I talked about for the next short piece of time. It was about us; it was probably foolish and loving.

And then the whole damned place seemed to blow up. I remember being knocked off my feet and wound up sitting on the floor, clinging to Shelda. The bedroom door burst open and Butler staggered out. Blood was streaming from a wound in his head, and he seemed to be dragging one leg behind him. He opened his mouth to say something and then fell flat on his face.

Hardy was at the door and I saw him turn away for a moment as though he was going to be sick. I got over to where he was and why I wasn't sick I will never know. The room was a shambles. There was a horrible bloody mess lying in the middle of the floor which I recognized as the remains of Allerton. Half of his head and one arm seemed to be missing.

A ghastly specter appeared in the bedroom door. It was George Battle.

Blood was running down his face. I saw that the mirror in the bathroom door was shattered. Battle pointed a shaking finger at Hardy.

"You sonofabitch!" he almost shrieked at the lieutenant. "You let this happen!"

I turned back into the living room to find Shelda. I didn't want her to see what was in the other room. I was just in time to see Chambrun come in the front door from the elevator. His face looked carved out of gray marble.

Part Three

1

THE next little bit of time is hazy in my memory. I guess we were all somewhat in shock. I remember Chambrun saying to me as he passed me on his way to the bedroom, "Call Partridge."

Dr. Partridge is the house physician. I remember hoping he wasn't too hungover. Doc gets plastered every night playing backgammon in the Spartan Bar with some cronies of his. As I put in the call, I remembered we had a doctor on the premises.

I saw Kranepool escorting a babbling George Battle into the living room and help him down into a corner of the couch. I was aware of the sweet, sickening smell of blood and something else, strong and pungent, which must have come from the explosive. Hardy appeared and I saw him kneel beside the unconscious Butler. And then Dr. Cobb put in an appearance. He headed straight for George Battle. One look and he disappeared, to return in half a minute with his medical bag.

All the time Battle was shouting accusations at Kranepool. It had been meant for him, he kept saying. The place was full of cops and they had let it happen. Only a miracle had saved him from a horrible death.

Nothing yet made the slightest sense to me. The place had been bombed out, but how? I remember going over to Shelda and taking her in my arms. She asked about Allerton.

"Blown to pieces," I said.

"Oh, God, Mark, if he hadn't taken in the mail for me — "

"Don't think about it, baby."

"If he hadn't done me a kindness because he knew I wanted to be here with you — " She buried her face against my shoulder. She was crying.

The mail turned out to be the key to the whole thing. It was a highly sophisticated device, contained in a letter, that had blown the room apart and sent the unhappy Allerton to join his ancestors. It was the same kind of device that Arab terrorists had made familiar in the preceding months in their attempts to murder Israeli diplomats and other important Jews in the world.

It was Chambrun, stone-faced, who finally got some kind of coherent story out of George Battle. The man had been in the bathroom doing something, as I understood it, about a denture that was bothering him. Allerton called to him from the bedroom saying that there was mail.

"I asked him if there was anything important," Battle told Chambrun. "He said there didn't seem to be. 'Except what looks like a birthday card for you, Mr. George'."

"Birthday card?" Chambrun asked.

"That's irony, isn't it?" Battle said. "Today is my birthday. I don't make a federal case out of it, Pierre. I was surprised that anyone knew — or cared. So I asked Allerton to open it and see who it was from. And — and the place blew up!"

Hardy had been on the phone to headquarters. "The bomb squad experts are on their way," he said. "I'm not sure, because it's not my specialty, that it was a letter bomb, but I don't see any other answer. I had reason to search that room thoroughly and I can promise you there wasn't any bomb planted there. There's no way to toss anything in from the roof. The windows in the bedroom and bathroom open onto the sheer wall of the building. Unless it was a letter bomb, Allerton or Butler had to be carrying the damn thing on them."

"It would have to be Allerton," Dr. Cobb said. He had gone over to the unconscious bodyguard. "This man and Mr. Battle were both hit by flying glass. I suspect Butler was knocked down by the impact of the explosion, which is how he hurt his leg. It would be helpful if I could get him moved to his room or some room — where I can stretch him out."

"What about the rest of the mail, George?" Chambrun asked Battle.

"I don't know what it is — or was," Battle said. "I told you, I was in the bathroom. A denture which age has forced on me was uncomfortable. I thought I must have fitted it into place improperly, so I went into the bathroom to fix it. I was standing, facing the mirror over the washbasin, when poor old Allerton called in and said there was mail. I told you that he said there didn't appear to be anything important. Then he mentioned the birthday card. I asked him to open it. That was that."

"I had the letters in my hands," Hardy said. "There were seven of them. Six of them looked like business letters — typewritten addresses, the names of business firms printed in the top left-hand corners. And there was a large, square green envelope, hand-addressed, that I assumed was some kind of a greeting card."

"Was there anything to indicate it was a birthday greeting?"

"No."

"So Allerton knew it was your birthday, George."

"For God sake, Pierre, Allerton has worked with me for nearly twenty years. I'm surprised that he remembered, poor devil, but of course he knew. And so, by the way, would anyone else who happened to look me up in *Who's Who*."

"What did you do with the letters, Hardy?" Chambrun asked.

"The detective who's riding the elevator brought them in," Hardy said. "I took them, shuffled through them for no particular reason, and took them to Miss Mason." He glanced at Shelda, who was still clinging to me. "I supposed, as Mr. Battle's secretary, she was the one to take them in."

Chambrun looked at me. "Allerton offered to take them," I said. "He knew

216

that Shelda and I — "

"What difference does it make who brought them in?" Battle asked, his voice shrill. "It was meant for me. If Allerton hadn't mentioned the birthday card, and I hadn't been involved in the bathroom, I would normally have opened the mail myself. I was curious when he mentioned a birthday card, so I asked him to open it. Ninety-nine times out of a hundred I would have opened it myself."

We watched while two of Hardy's men picked up the unconscious bodyguard and carried him down the hall, followed by Dr. Cobb.

"The force of the explosion was terrific," Battle said. "If I hadn't been standing by the washbasin and able to grab it for support, it would have knocked me down. The mirror above it shattered and that's what cut my face. The mirror behind me in the door also shattered. I heard Ed Butler screaming and I staggered to the door and saw — saw Allerton. Christ Almighty!"

"Butler was in your room when Allerton came in with the mail?"

"Of course he was there. Do you think I'd leave myself unprotected for five seconds after what had already happened here? You and your damned security people, Pierre, and the lieutenant and his stupid cops haven't been very much use to me up to now. I had to have somebody I trusted with me, and now one of them is dead and the other only alive, like me, by some miracle. Pierre, what are you going to do to stop the next attempt?" Battle stared at Chambrun for a moment and then leaned back against the couch, looking exhausted. He blotted at a little trickle of blood that ran down his cheek.

Chambrun stood very still for a moment, obviously not intending to answer Battle's question. Then he turned to me. "We're going to have to find different quarters for Mr. Battle," he said. "Find out from Atterbury exactly what's available. Not on the fourteenth floor, please. I don't want him near Cleaves, Potter and Company." I started to head for the front door, but he stopped it. "Talk to Atterbury on the house phone," he said. "We're going to have to go into a huddle over what's to be done with the press." He turned to Shelda. "That house phone is going to start ringing steadily in a moment. No way that explosion can stay a secret. Are you up to manning it, Shelda? We talk to no one except people who want Hardy or Kranepool from their headquarters. For anyone else the answer is no, unless you make some special judgment on it."

"I can manage it," Shelda said.

"Good girl. Hardy, I think we should talk to Butler if Dr. Cobb has brought him around."

★ ★ ★

Ed Butler had come out of it when I joined Chambrun, Hardy, and Kranepool in the bodyguard's bedroom down the hall. He wasn't

219

the cold, tough cookie he had been the night before. He looked as if he'd been crying. He was propped up against the pillows on his bed, and there was a surgical patch above his left temple.

"He's not seriously hurt," Dr. Cobb was telling the others as I came in. "I took eight stitches in that scalp wound. When the explosion knocked him down, he twisted his knee. It's going to bother him for a while. There's some hysterical shock involved." It came out of Cobb between little gasps for breath.

"Where were you, Doctor, when the blast went off?" Chambrun asked.

"In my room. Breathing. Oxygen. It damn near rolled me out of bed. My God, a small thing in a letter could do all that damage?"

"You saw for yourself," Chambrun said. "Can Butler talk to us?"

"Why not?" the doctor said.

Chambrun moved to the edge of the bed and looked down at Butler. "Tell us exactly what happened in the bedroom, Mr. Butler."

Butler moistened his lips. "I — I was in there, sitting in a chair by the window, when Allerton came in. He had some letters in his hand. He looked around for Mr. Battle and I told him the old boy was in the bathroom. The bathroom door was open, so whatever he was doing clearly wasn't private. Allerton was looking at the letters. He held up a large green envelope. 'Someone's sent the old effer a birthday card', he said. I walked over to him and we stood looking at the envelope. Not many people feel sentimental about Mr. Battle. We were both wondering who it could be, I guess. Then Allerton took a few steps away from me and called in to the old man. Told him there was mail. The old man asked him if there was anything that looked important. Allerton said no, but there was a birthday card for him. The old man sounded surprised and told Allerton to open it. I — I told you he'd taken a few steps away from me — Allerton, I mean — and I guess that saved my life. He started to open the envelope and the place blew up. I was knocked flat and I felt something tear into my head. It was glass from the window, I think. I tried to stand up and my knee felt like a knife was in it. Then — then I saw what was left of Allerton and I got the hell out of there."

It checked exactly with what Battle had told us.

Chambrun was frowning. "Do you know, Mr. Butler, who gave instructions to have mail brought up here?"

"How do you mean?"

"I ask because it isn't normal routine for mail to be delivered to the rooms unless there are special instructions to that effect."

"It wouldn't be me," Butler said. "Miss Mason or Allerton would handle that kind of job."

Chambrun turned to the house phone beside the bed and asked for Mr. Atterbury on the front desk. "Atterbury? Chambrun here. You sent mail up to the penthouse this morning? — So find out. — You didn't have a routine request to have mail sent up? — Thank you." Chambrun put down the phone. "The desk had no instructions. You say it was one of your men who delivered the mail up here, Hardy?"

"Detective Pagano," Hardy said. "He's stationed on the special elevator."

"It might be a good idea to find out how he came by it," Chambrun said. He turned back to Butler as Hardy went out of the room. "You are hired, Butler, as a bodyguard. How long have you had the job?"

"Twelve years this summer," Butler said.

"How many times in those twelve years has some kind of attack been made on Mr. Battle?"

Butler hesitated. "For real, not till last night," he said.

"You mean when the man in the stocking mask took a shot at him?"

"That's it. But you have to know

that this trip to New York is the first time he's left the villa in Cannes since I worked for him. Oh, we've had people try to get into the grounds over there; reporters trying to interview him, photographers hoping to get a shot of him. I've had to throw them out, drive them off. But when you say 'attack' I suppose you mean someone trying to do him harm. Last night was the first time."

"Tend to make you rather careless, wouldn't it?" Chambrun asked, quite casual.

"You don't work for Mr. Battle and get careless," Butler said.

"But when you saw all the precautions that were set up last night, you must have thought it was pretty absurd. It would keep out the press, and the curious Peeping Toms, but you didn't think someone would try to get to him to kill him. Or did you?"

"Mr. Battle made a big point of it," Butler said. "It was the first time he'd come out of his own — his own like fortress — for seventeen years. He told us there were people all over the world who might try to get at him. He didn't leave any doubt that he expected trouble."

"But you didn't expect it, which is why you fell asleep at your post?"

Butler pushed himself up on his elbows, and he winced as pain hit him somewhere. *"I did not fall asleep!"* he almost shouted. He lowered himself, and his voice was unsteady as he went on. "Sure, I might have dozed off in the garden back home — Cannes. There is an electric fence, and guards at the gates. Anyone tries to sneak in there and it sounds like the Fourth of July. Bells ring, sirens start screaming. But here there were no alarms and I stayed awake."

"And no one went into that bedroom?"

"Absolutely no one!"

"And yet there was someone there. The man in the stocking mask got in there somehow."

"I know. And I don't know how,"

Butler said. "He didn't get by me is all I do know."

Hardy came back into the room. He was frowning. "Some guy handed the letters to Pagano," he said, "and told him Mr. Battle had asked to have them brought up. Pagano supposed he was someone connected with the hotel. Business suit, no hat. The elevator operator saw him, didn't know him, supposed he was a cop. About six feet, medium brown hair, blue or grey eyes, maybe thirty — thirty-five years old. They both say they'd know him again. Maybe we can get a police artist to do a makeup on him. Pagano and the elevator operator both took it for granted. It didn't seem odd Mr. Battle would want his mail. At the desk they say there was no mail to send up. Never was any."

"Neat," Chambrun said. The corner of his mouth moved in a tight smile. "Going to make an unhappy story for you, friend, when the press gets hold of it. The bomb which killed the wrong man was delivered by a police detective." He turned back to Butler. "Some time ago, in Cannes, Maxie Zorn came to visit Mr. Battle. With him were Peter Potter, who had once worked for Battle, and Richard Cleaves. The appointment was with Zorn. The other two weren't admitted until George — Mr. Battle — had given you the green light. Right?"

"Right. But afterwards — "

"Afterwards you were ordered not to let Cleaves inside the grounds again. How about Potter?"

"You got to understand something," Butler said. "No one was ever let in without an okay from Mr. Battle — not even his mother if he had one. There were no old friends who just dropped in. The thing that was different about Cleaves — well, Mr. Battle acted real scared of him. He seemed to think he might have some trick for getting in. He said — and this sounds crazy — that if he, Mr. Battle, was to tell me, right to my face, to let Cleaves in, I wasn't to do it. It didn't make any sense, but I kept an eye out for Cleaves."

"He didn't show again?"

"No. Then I heard he was here in the hotel. That's another reason I effing well didn't fall asleep on the job last night."

That seemed to be all there was to get from Butler. An all-around pretty odd story. When we got back to the sitting room, Jerry Dodd was there. He was talking to Shelda over by the phone. Battle was still sitting on the couch, with two cops standing directly behind him. Jerry joined us.

"Christ, what a mess here," he said.

"You find out anything?" Chambrun asked.

"For what it's worth. The room you were held in, boss, was rented for a week in advance by a man named Smith. What else! About six feet tall, the landlady says; blue eyes, light brown hair, maybe thirty-five years old."

Chambrun and Hardy exchanged glances. The letter man.

"The old lady is something of a lush," Jerry said. "Spends most of her time in a basement apartment sucking on a gin bottle. This Smith character paid her in cash and she says she never saw him again. Never happened to run into him in the building. She had no reason to check on him because he still had four days to go on his advance payment. She isn't curious as long as the gin holds out. So maybe we have a kind of description of Stocking Mask."

"Twice over," Hardy said, and told Jerry about the mail deliverer.

"Maybe you'll find fingerprints on the letters," Jerry said.

Hardy didn't brighten. "Have you looked in the other room?" he asked.

Then the doorbell rang and the people from the bomb squad were there.

★ ★ ★

A little later we had a report from Captain Carlson of the bomb squad. From the bits and pieces they'd been able to sweep up there was no doubt it was a letter bomb.

"A very sophisticated piece of equipment," Carlson said. He was an efficient-looking gray-haired man in his late fifties. I learned later he'd spent most of World War II in the army, defusing live bombs that had fallen on the city of London and either failed to go off, or were equipped with delayed firing mechanisms. He had spent most of his life, seconds from death, working with a watchmaker's precision to save his own life and thousands of others. He knew all there was to know about bombs, large and small.

"It had to be put together by an expert," Carlson told us. "This was no homemade piece of junk that kids might build. It had to take pretty rough handling — travel in the mail, tossed around by the deliverer. It would only go off when the flap was ripped open, theoretically by the person it was addressed to. Ordinarily no one opens a birthday card except the birthday boy."

"The letters were faked," Hardy said. "By that I mean they didn't come through the regular mail delivery to the hotel. I saw them before the explosion. They were addressed to the hotel; they appeared to have postmarks. I mean, nothing looked odd about them. But we know they didn't come through the mail to the hotel."

"I don't know what we can produce for you," Carlson said. "That poor devil in there was evidently holding all the letters in his hands when he opened the birthday card. The force of the explosion blew off his arm and half of his head and all that's left of the letters is a charred mass of paper — only one or two unburned pieces. They don't look promising. There are enough tiny scraps of metal for us to identify the kind of bomb it was, but nothing that could have fingerprints or anything else helpful."

George Battle had been listening very intently to Carlson's report. A little nerve kept twitching around the cut on his cheek.

"This man has failed twice to get me, Pierre," he said.

"Failed first by a matter of inches, failed the second time by what he must consider an extraordinary piece of bad luck. The first time he walked past your men and my bodyguard, even though they were supposedly on the alert. Now Allerton, who protected me from the possibility of other subtle forms of attack, like poison, has died in my place. The police are here" — and he waved his hand in a derisive gesture at Hardy and his men — "but they never prevent anything from happening. They may catch my murderer after I am dead, which is very little comfort to me. And this explosives genius can tell us all about the bomb — after it has exploded. So, Pierre, what are you going to do to find this man before he gets me? I know you will try, perhaps not because you are fond of me, but because this man is giving your beloved hotel an incredibly bad reputation. When this bomb story gets public, people are going to start checking out of the Beaumont like rats leaving a ship."

"We'll do what we can, George," Chambrun said in a flat voice.

"That's not good enough! In the old days, Pierre, you could plan a campaign. Have you lost your touch? Have you, unhappily, grown old? If I can't count on you, God help me."

Believe it or not, Chambrun smiled at him. "Your helpless-baby act may impress the others, George, but not me. In all the years I've known you, I've never been able to beat you at a single game of chess, and I'm not a bad player. You are the best planner, the best schemer I know. So tell us what to do, George, because I'm sure you're way, way ahead of us at this point. We can't help you if you keep secrets from us, you know."

2

THESE two old friends looked at each other, and they were both smiling now. Thirty years ago they had fought together, perhaps for different motives, to save a dying nation. Violence, like the violence in the other room which had made me sick and weak in the knees, was no stranger to them. I thought of Chambrun's twenty friends cut down in the basement of the St. Germaine house, and later St. Germaine hanging from a lamppost outside that house. They weren't smiling because of anything in the present, but because they were remembering the life-and-death games they'd played together in the past, remembering their skills which must have been very different. Battle's weapons were wealth and power and influence which he could very well have handled with a kind of Machiavellian competence. Chambrun's must have been the quick mind, the physical courage, the ability to cut through to the very center of a problem without ever being sidetracked.

"If you will tell us some of the things we don't know, George, we'll be a lot better able to help you," Chambrun said. He tapped one of his flat Egyptian cigarettes on the back of his hand before he lit it, his eyes narrowed against the smoke.

It was a strange moment. Hardy, Kranepool, and Jerry and I were circling the two friends, with Shelda a little way off at the phone. Behind us men came and went; men from the bomb squad, men from Homicide, because Hardy really had a murder now. And finally I was aware of men carrying a stretcher with a sheet covering what was left of Allerton. Cobb was still with Ed Butler in the rear bedroom, and somewhere, probably in the kitchen, was Gaston, the chef. It was a busy place, and yet it somehow seemed to me that there were only two people there — Chambrun and George Battle.

"What is it you want me to tell you that you don't know, Pierre?" Battle asked. He was leaning back against the couch, holding a handkerchief to the cut on his cheek. His blue eyes seemed to have lighted up with a kind of excitement. He and Chambrun are playing an old, familiar game, I thought, and it has brought him to life.

"What are you doing here in New York, at the Beaumont, to start with?" Chambrun said.

"It's my hotel," Battle said. I thought he said it to annoy Chambrun. Chambrun is the hotel; he has made it what it is, a way of life. Battle owned the real estate, that was all.

"Not good enough, George," Chambrun said, still smiling. "For seventeen years you have lived behind the walls of your own fortress in Cannes. You have lived in fear of an attack on your life. I know what most people don't know, George — that it is not a form of hypochondria. You have a right to be afraid. You have earned the undying hatred of too many people. Yet you suddenly come away from your safe place, cross an ocean, set yourself up where you are wide open to attack."

"Not wide open," Battle said. "I had every reason to think I would be as safe here, under your protection, as I could be anywhere else."

"Let's not play games with each other, George. The risk here had to be greater. You took it for a reason. If I knew what that reason was it might be useful."

"I have a great many million dollars invested in this hotel," Battle said. "I thought it was time I came to see how things are here."

Chambrun wasn't smiling any more. He turned to me. "Let's go, Mark. We have the press to deal with and a hotel to get back on an even keel." He started for the door.

"Wait, Pierre!" Battle's voice had a note of pleading in it.

Chambrun looked back at him. "I don't have time to play games with you, George. The police can protect you. I have a hotel to run."

"Please. Let's try again, Pierre. I couldn't resist needling you. You're right, of course. My enemies are legion."

"There are too goddam many of them," Chambrun said. "But exposing yourself to two of them as you have doesn't make sense. Why are you involved in a deal that includes Richard Cleaves and Peter Potter, two gilt-edged enemies of yours? You're not interested in making motion pictures. These two men hate your guts, and yet you play at making a business deal that involves them, and you move into the same hotel with them. Let's start with making sense out of that, George."

Battle was silent for a moment. "Have you read *A Man's World* by Richard Cleaves, Pierre?"

"No."

"Take time to skim through the first fifty pages," Battle said. "When you have, you will understand my interest in it."

"Interest in having it produced because you think it's a work of art?" Chambrun asked.

"Interest in not having it produced," Battle said. His bright eyes looked past Chambrun to the rest of us. "You understand, gentlemen, what I am saying is off the record. You understand, Pierre, I didn't know who Richard Cleaves was when I picked up the book. When I had read it, I saw a notice in the Paris *Tribune* that Maxwell Zorn had optioned the book for a film production. I had to stop the book being filmed, or at least control what the final shooting script was to be."

"Why, George?" Chambrun was obviously puzzled.

"Read the first fifty pages, Pierre. At first I thought it was one of those strange coincidences; the inventive mind of a storyteller had hit on something that paralleled something that had happened in real life, down to the last detail. Something you will recognize, Pierre, that was part of my life. It was quite possible that a popular work of fiction might not fall into certain hands. But make it into a film that will be seen all over the world, a film starring a popular star like David Loring, and the wrong people would be certain to see it. I had to stop it, or control it, change certain details of the story. I cabled Maxwell Zorn and offered to put up the money for the film. He came running, bringing the author with him, and his public relations man — my old friend Peter Potter. Potter doesn't frighten me, Pierre. He is just a disgruntled ex-employee. I was interested to meet the author, whose imagination had paralleled my life so closely. Cleaves didn't attempt to hide the truth about himself when he came to my house with Zorn. He hadn't been in the room with me three minutes, hiding behind those damned black glasses, when he said to me, cool as you please, 'My real name is Richard St. Germaine'. Then I knew. His book wasn't pure fiction, accidentally copying my life. It was the result of careful research. It was a diabolical scheme for personal revenge. He wouldn't have to lift a finger. When the right people saw the film, they would kill me. They could and they would."

"What people?" Hardy asked.

"Sorry, Lieutenant. All I can tell you is that they are not here in New York; that they haven't been involved in what has happened so far."

"And yet you've come here, making yourself a much easier target," Chambrun said.

"A lesson I learned from you long ago, Pierre," Battle said. "When someone is hunting you, don't run. You always used to say that, friend. Force his hand. Make him attack. He'll have to come out in the open and you'll be ready for him. So I came here, feeling certain Cleaves would make a try for me and that I'd have him. I didn't think he'd strike the first night. I thought he'd have to scout out the territory. I had intended to alert you, Pierre, after I'd had a night's rest. But he moved too soon for me, and as you can see, if he can't get at me one way, he'll find another."

"Hold it, Mr. Battle," Jerry Dodd said. "He has a perfect alibi for the time you were shot at. Miss Mason was with him, along with two other witnesses. And are you suggesting that he's the one who kidnaped Mr. Chambrun?"

"He could have been."

"Impossible," Jerry said. "He had an alibi for that time, too."

Battle's eyes narrowed. "Provided by the same two witnesses who covered for him the first time — David Loring and Angela Adams. Too many perfect alibis become no alibi at all, Mr. Dodd."

"He could have sent you a birthday

card at Cannes just as readily as here," Chambrun said.

"But I was here," Battle said.

"He could have sent it any time during the last ten years," Chambrun said.

"That's unlikely, Mr. Chambrun," Captain Carlson, the bomb expert, said. "We haven't known much about the technique of these letter bombs until relatively recently. The Arabs began to use them against the Israelis about a year — eighteen months — ago. Before that bombs came in the mail, to be sure, but in packages. You can suspect an unordered package. But these letter things — well, unless you're expecting them, they're almost impossible to detect until it's too late. Unheard of ten years ago."

"That's nit-picking, Captain," Battle said. "The fact is the letter came this morning, and damn near did what it was intended to do." He drew a deep breath. "I came here, inviting attack so I could catch him at it. He turns out to be much cleverer than I had foreseen."

"Proof?" Hardy asked, looking like a puzzled basset hound.

"That's your job. Let me point out one thing to you, Lieutenant. Perhaps his alibis will hold up. That would be clever, wouldn't it? He didn't actually fire the shot at me. In this day and age you don't have to do the deed yourself, Mr. Hardy. I have run an empire from inside the fences of my place in Cannes. Someone else does the actual leg work, but I plan it. Cleaves, unless he's an unexpected genius, didn't make that bomb himself. He hired someone to make it for him. He probably hired someone to take a shot at me. Why do you suppose Pierre was kidnaped?"

"I'll bite," Hardy said.

"Because he needed money to finance his war against me," Battle laughed. "Ironic, isn't it? I pay for the plan and the weapons that are meant to destroy me."

I remembered something Chambrun

had said the night before, when Shelda had given Cleaves his alibi for the time of the shooting at Battle. "The finger that squeezes the trigger isn't necessarily attached to the brain that plans the action."

"You're accusing Cleaves, then?" Hardy asked.

"I accuse him of being the planner," Battle said. "But let me tell you something. You can arrest him on suspicion, put him in jail, and you'll only provide him with an alibi for the next move against me. What you have to find out, if you're going to do me any good, Lieutenant, is who is his trigger man? Who is his bomb expert?"

There was a moment of silence.

"There are things about your own scheme I don't understand, George," Chambrun finally said. He lit a fresh cigarette. He turned to look toward the phones. "Shelda, for one. Why have you made her playing a nude scene in the film a condition for your financing?"

Battle glanced at Shelda, smiling. "Because I am a very shrewd and very wicked old man," he said. "I needed time and I thought I knew Shelda well enough to count on the certainty that she would say no," at least until Zorn's offer became so astronomical she couldn't refuse. I insisted on having five prints of the film. I knew they'd assume I expected to get some kind of sexual jolt out of watching Shelda perform in the raw with Loring." He gestured toward Shelda. "Believe me, my dear, decrepit and ancient as I may appear to you, only the real thing would give me the slightest satisfaction."

I stuck in my oar for the first time. I didn't like the way the old man was leering at Shelda. "According to Cleaves, you have fixed it so that no one else will finance the film," I said.

"That is momentarily true," Battle said. "As long as I am actually interested, he won't find any other financing. But, as the old saying goes, if I don't get off the pot pretty soon, someone will make an offer. So I will, in the end, have to agree to the financing in order to control the script, get the changes made that must be made. I'll only get that concession from Zorn when he is desperate. But beyond a certain point someone will offer him a way out. Right now" — and he pointed a finger at Hardy — "I'm more concerned with saving my life than dealing with Zorn. If Cleaves gets to me, it won't matter about the film. I can only be dead once."

I thought Chambrun had other questions, but he evidently changed his mind about asking them. "We're going to have to move you out of here, George," he said. "This place isn't livable, and it obviously isn't safe. We'll put you in another suite, with Hardy's men or Jerry's occupying the rooms on either side of you. The halls will be covered. There's no possible way for Cleaves to know in advance where you're going — because I don't know myself at this moment. There can't be any advance booby traps for you."

"What about Edward Butler?" Battle asked. "Is he in shape to stand by?"

"Whether he's in shape or not, Jerry Dodd isn't going to let you out of his sight," Chambrun said. "Our friend with the stocking mask seems to have been invisible to Butler. Jerry's eyesight is infallible. I do have one more question to ask you, George. How do you account for the fact that the shot of sedative which Dr. Cobb said would knock you out for twelve hours didn't work?"

Battle actually grinned. "It wasn't a shot, if you mean by that an injection," Battle said.

"Pills?"

"Yes."

Chambrun nodded slowly. "And you didn't take them," he said.

Battle was obviously delighted with himself. "Cobb thought he saw me take them, but of course I didn't," he said. "You don't suppose I was going to let myself be knocked out when there was a killer waiting for just such an opportunity, do you?"

★ ★ ★

We left the penthouse with Jerry staying behind as Battle's special bodyguard. We headed for the office with Hardy and Kranepool coming with us. Plans had to be made.

As we walked into Miss Ruysdale's outer office, she got up from her desk and handed Chambrun a book. It was *A Man's World* by Richard Cleaves.

"I thought you might be wanting this," she said.

She could set up as a psychic, I thought.

In his office Chambrun, who'd shown no surprise at being handed the book, asked us to excuse him for a moment while he made some necessary arrangements by phone. He knew how to play it close to the vest. He talked, first, to Atterbury on the front desk. A suite was available on the seventeenth floor, and by checkout time the two rooms on either side of the suite would be available.

"No one is to know that Mr. Battle is occupying that suite," Chambrun said. "Mrs. Kniffin is the housekeeper on that floor. She is to be told nothing about the occupant of the suite, except that he doesn't want the suite serviced. Battle will not be registered. The office is only to know that I am holding those rooms. The switchboard, if asked, is simply to say that Mr. Battle is no longer registered here. That will be a fact, so the operators won't need any special instructions. There will be a DO NOT DISTURB on the suite, which means that no calls will be put through, even though someone simply asks for the room number, unless there are special instructions from me or Jerry. I will let you know exactly when Battle is to be moved down. It will be when we are quite sure people we are concerned with are occupied. All clear? — Thank you, Atterbury."

Chambrun leaned back in his desk chair. He reached for the cup of Turkish coffee Ruysdale had placed within reach.

"You want me to stay, Mr. Chambrun?" she asked.

"Please, Ruysdale," he said. His smile was bitter. "In case I should disappear again, you'd better know what the score is."

"You buy this Cleaves theory?" Kranepool asked.

"It could very well be," Chambrun said. "Cleaves has a motive. Potter might be willing to help him. Potter knows exactly how George's mind works. George is right, of course. You can hire killers and experts. He's also right in assuming that coming out of his private fortress he could flush his killer into the open — Cleaves, his hired hands, or someone we haven't even thought of yet." He glanced at the bright jacket on Cleaves' novel. "I'm going to have to find time to look at this. My theory is, Hardy, that you have perfectly good grounds now for holding Cleaves and Potter for questioning. You have a murder. That letter bomb makes alibis for any special time meaningless. You don't know when it was made, when it was mailed. I suggest you bring Cleaves and Potter down here. While you're holding them, Battle can be moved to his new quarters. And while they're here, we should arrange for the detective and the operator who were on the elevator and took the mail from our mystery man in the lobby to have a look at Cleaves. I think it's unlikely, but he just could be the man."

"Not Potter?" Kranepool asked.

"You're not aware, Kranepool, that Potter is a dwarf, not quite four feet tall?" Chambrun asked.

★ ★ ★

As I have suggested, the story of the explosion in the penthouse had spread. People in the other two penthouses and on the two floors below the roof had actually heard and felt it. The switchboard had been swamped with calls. Bombs seem to be a part of today's climate; bomb threats are so frequent that people are almost indifferent to them. I can't tell you how many times I've found myself walking along a city street, a popular busy avenue like Madison, or Fifth, or Park and seen an abnormal number of people crowded around a corner. You look for what you suppose has been an accident and you see none. Then you ask, and someone tells you, quite casually, as though it was every day, that people have been evacuated from the building across the way because of a bomb threat. Public schools are constant targets for bombing sorties by idiot teen-agers. It is all part of an age of terror that is crippling our cities and even our rural communities. The usual explanations are 'radicals' or 'racists'. The frightening thing about it is that, while people stay home at night because they feel the streets aren't safe, the bombing thing is everywhere, from the United Nations to the Staten Island Ferry terminal, and people allow themselves to be herded away from the danger area like sheep, and then go back when they get the all-clear, still like sheep.

I wasn't in on Battle's move from the penthouse to his new quarters on the seventeenth floor, and therefore I wasn't in on the beginning of the session in Chambrun's office with Cleaves and Potter. I had to deal once more with the press and with dozens of guests who wanted assurances from Chambrun and nobody else that it was still safe to stay in the hotel.

The bomb had gone off in the penthouse about eleven o'clock. It was nearly twelve-thirty when I left Chambrun's office and went downstairs to undertake my part of the job. I learned afterwards that at about one-thirty Battle had been moved, along with Cobb, Butler, Gaston, and, somewhat to my dismay, Shelda. I wanted her out of there, away from the center of trouble, but, knowing her, I knew she'd stick with Battle as long as he wanted her to. People on the seventeenth floor must have guessed something was up. The corridors were patrolled by men who had cop written all over them. Cobb, Butler, Gaston, and Shelda were moved down first, accompanied by Jerry's men. When they were safely in, Battle himself was brought down, surrounded by Jerry and a half dozen plainclothes men. An elevator was commandeered for the purpose, and I don't think many people saw it happen.

Just before the exodus from the roof started, Hardy had picked up Cleaves and Potter and brought them down to Chambrun's office. There was no way they could know exactly where Battle had been taken unless, and it seemed possible, Cleaves had somebody watching for him. I knew, later, that when Cleaves was brought down to the office, the detective who had brought up the mail and the elevator operator who had run the penthouse car had been given an opportunity to get a good look at him. He was not, they both said without any question, the man who had delivered the letters which had included the birthday greeting.

It took me forever, it seemed, to satisfy the men from the newspapers and the TV and radio stations. There was no way to evade the truth this time. Yes, there had been a second attempt on George Battle's life. Yes, a so-called letter bomb, addressed to Battle, had been opened by Battle's valet and the man was dead. No, there was no reason to think there was any danger to anyone else in the hotel, no reason to think that public areas in the hotel were in any danger of being bombed.

My friend from the *News* threw me another curve. "Is it true, Mark, that Pierre Chambrun is among the missing?"

"Not true. He's in his office now."

"Can we get a statement from him?"

"Not now."

"*Was* he among the missing?" my *News* friend persisted.

"He was out of the hotel for a few hours," I said.

"Come on, Mark, it's all around that he was kidnaped and that a ransom was paid to get him free. True or false? And has the ransom been paid and is he free?"

"He's in his office now, consulting with the police on the best way to protect Mr. Battle," I said, ducking. All we needed to start a panic was to confirm the fact that Chambrun himself had been in trouble.

I finally got out of there with a whole skin and headed upstairs to Chambrun's office. Cleaves and Potter were with him, along with Miss Ruysdale, Hardy, and Kranepool. I hesitated in the doorway.

"Come in, Mark," Chambrun said. He was leaning back in his desk chair, his dark eyes buried deep in their pouches. "I think you know both Mr. Cleaves and Mr. Potter."

I said, "Hi!"

It didn't look like a rubber-hose third degree had been going on. Both men had coffee cups on side tables beside their chairs. Potter gave me his mischievous smile, looking as though he was having a ball. Cleaves, hidden behind those black glasses, gave me a curt nod. Without waiting for an invitation I went over to the sideboard and poured myself a slug of Jack Daniels.

Kranepool was evidently handling this part of the interrogation. He didn't look as bright and fresh as he had twelve hours ago.

"You don't deny, Cleaves, that you've dreamed most of your life of getting revenge for what happened to your father, and that Mr. Battle and Mr. Chambrun were your prime targets?"

"I don't deny it," Cleaves said in

his flat, cold voice. The black glasses turned my way. "Didn't Haskell tell you I've actually had Mr. Chambrun in the sights of a gun but I couldn't, for some reason, pull the trigger? Didn't he also tell you that I assured him that if I was ever lucky enough to find Battle available that I wouldn't have any qualms?"

"Then you must see that I have no choice but to hold you on suspicion of murder."

"I'd think you were an idiot if you didn't," Cleaves said. "I'd feel very much better if you did, because when it's tried again, I'd have the perfect alibi."

Chambrun stirred in his chair. "The whereabouts of your physical body, Mr. Cleaves, isn't very important to us. We know you didn't fire the shot at George Battle last night. There is nothing in your history to suggest that you are an expert in the field of explosives. If you are guilty of these two attempts on Battle's life, it is as an employer of an assassin and a bomb expert."

"That will take some proving," Cleaves said, undisturbed.

Chambrun reached out and put his hand down on the copy of *A Man's World* which lay in front of him on the desk. "I haven't read this, Mr. Cleaves, a deficiency which I expect to remedy in a short while. What is there about it that so interests and disturbs George Battle?"

"I wish to God I knew," Cleaves said. "You know him, Chambrun. You know how devious he is. I've never thought he wanted to finance the film. Quite the contrary, I think he wants to stop its being made. He's kept us dangling for nearly a month with absurd conditions. He's managed to block other ways of getting money. Knowing him, I'm certain he has no intention of financing us."

"He's admitted that to us," Chambrun said.

Cleaves was suddenly animated. He

leaned forward in his chair. "Why, for God sake?"

"That he hasn't told us. I assumed you could."

"I haven't the faintest idea."

Potter laughed, wriggling in his chair, his short legs dangling above the floor. "Maybe Richard has ESP," he said. "Maybe he revealed something in his book about Battle without knowing he was doing it."

"That's pure crap, Peter," Cleaves said. "If I had something on Battle, I wouldn't hide it in a fiction story. I'd let him have it right between the eyes."

"You want him dead," Kranepool said:

"Would you have a love affair with the man who paid to have your father killed?" Cleaves asked.

"Or with the man who killed him?" Chambrun's voice was quiet. "Your motive is so clear-cut, Cleaves."

"As far as you are concerned, Chambrun, I had my chances at

you and for some reason, God knows what, I couldn't go through with it. Perhaps if I got my chance at Battle, the same thing would happen. Perhaps I'm simply not a killer when the chips are down."

"But if you could damage him with your book — ?"

"I would, and glory in it. But, so help me, I don't know what there is in my novel that disturbs him."

"What about you, Potter?" Kranepool asked. "You worked for him, you hated him, you quit him."

"He laughed at my deformity," Potter said. "I hated his guts for that. But killing him wouldn't take the hump off my back or make me six feet tall."

"So you quit him?" Kranepool asked. He went on without waiting for an answer. "There are strange responses to Mr. Battle. People hate him, fear him, and yet the people who work close to him seem to be unusually faithful. Allerton had worked for him for twenty years; Dr. Cobb about the same length of time; Butler, the bodyguard, for something more than twelve; Gaston, the chef, for eight. That suggests he isn't too bad to work for below the surface. They stand by him, and he counts on them completely."

Potter laughed. "None of you, unless it's Mr. Chambrun, really understand George Battle," he said. "He doesn't count on love and kisses to get what he wants. I'll bet my best silk undershirt Allerton and Cobb and the others haven't stood by him all this time out of gratitude or affection."

"Meaning what?" Kranepool asked.

"Meaning Battle has something on them," Potter said. "If anything happens to Battle, these people will all go into a carefully prepared meat grinder. I'll bet if you go back in their histories — and I'm just guessing, you understand — you'll find the good Dr. Cobb was guilty of some sort of malpractice which would put him in jail for the rest of his life; the others have some kind of ax hanging over their heads. Battle counts on them because he can destroy them if their feet slip."

Kranepool looked at Chambrun.

"Interesting theory," Chambrun said. "George doesn't ordinarily leave anything to chance." He put out his cigarette in the ash tray on his desk. "I find myself still interested in your book, Mr. Cleaves, and the film script. Are there changes and additions in the film script that don't appear in the novel?"

Cleaves shrugged. "The much-talked-about nude scene," he said. "That's added for box office purposes. Actually Peter suggested it."

Potter chuckled. "We've gotten a lot of mileage out of it so far," he said. "There hasn't been as much interest in a casting project since they were trying to get someone to play Scarlett O'Hara."

"Other changes?" Chambrun asked.

"A few minor plot gimmicks that tighten the story. In a novel you can explain things in narration; in a film the explanation has to be visual."

"Would it be possible for me to read the film script in addition to the book?" Chambrun asked.

"Why not," Cleaves said. He leaned forward in his chair. "Does Battle think I'm the one who's out to get him? Because if he does, I'm entitled to a little protection, gentlemen."

"Protection?" Hardy said.

"If Battle thinks I'm responsible for the shot that was taken at him, and the bombing, he may not wait around for you to solve the case, Lieutenant. George Battle fights his own wars."

"Nobody is going to fight any wars," Hardy said. "Mr. Battle is being guarded by my men and the hotel security. He won't move anywhere without our people around him. That's meant to protect him, but it will also protect you, Cleaves, if you are in any danger."

"Those could be famous last words," Potter said, and he giggled.

3

CLEAVES and Potter were returned to their rooms with instructions from Kranepool not to leave the hotel without his permission. They were, in effect, being held for questioning without being made uncomfortable. Kranepool took off for the penthouse where the rubble in the bedroom was still being sifted and examined by Carlson and his men. Postal inspectors were trying to trace the letters that had been delivered to the penthouse. From Hardy's evidence there was no question they'd been addressed to Battle and apparently postmarked in the normal fashion.

Hardy seemed reluctant to leave us.

"We don't have a hell of a lot to go on," he said to Chambrun. "If you're right, and the principal in the case is hiring some outsider, or outsiders, to do the job, we don't have a single lead. It must have been all carefully planned before Battle ever arrived in the hotel — a way to get into the penthouse, the letter bomb isn't something you put together in a few minutes. With the kind of security we've thrown around Battle, do you think there'll be another try?"

"You think kidnaping me was planned before Battle arrived here?" Chambrun asked. His eyes were narrowed, looking past Hardy to somewhere.

"Like we said, a way to raise money to pay for the project," Hardy said. "Whoever we're dealing with knows Battle well enough to know he'd come through with ransom money for you."

"But how well informed this character is," Chambrun said. "The shot was taken at Battle, the police and the assistant D.A. arrived. Who knew that you were in charge of the case except those of us who were in the penthouse, Hardy?"

Hardy shrugged. "I came through the

lobby. People in the hotel know me. I've been here before, you know."

"And Kranepool? Who could know in advance the name of the assistant D.A.? It was a phone call, supposedly from him, that trapped me. Only somebody in that penthouse knew Kranepool's name."

"He made calls in and out," Hardy said. "Someone on your switchboard? It could have happened that way, you know. 'I want to speak to the assistant D.A. — What's his name'? Your operator tells the caller. No reason not to."

"Could be," Chambrun said. He looked at me. "Have Ruysdale check out if there was such a call, Mark."

I went to the outer office and gave Miss Ruysdale the word. Hardy and Chambrun were still at it when I rejoined them.

"You're saying that only someone in the penthouse would have known the assistant D.A.'s name," Hardy was saying. "I said, in the beginning, that only someone in the penthouse could have fired that shot at Battle. But none of the four men in the penthouse had a gun. I searched them, like I said, right down to their skins. I searched their rooms, the entire apartment. No gun."

"And none of them could have been my man in the stocking mask," Chambrun said.

"So there is more than one Stocking Mask," Hardy said.

"There can be an army of them if it's a paid job being done by outsiders," Chambrun said. "But how were these outsiders made aware of the assistant D.A.'s name?"

"They could have seen him come. They could have been watching in the lobby when he arrived and known him by sight. They can be watching everything we do right now, damn it!"

"I think I'd like to talk with Dr. Cobb," Chambrun said. "Maybe he was joking when he said he knew how Stocking Mask got into the penthouse. Maybe he wasn't."

I was sent up to the seventeenth floor to ask Dr. Cobb to come down to the boss's office. I didn't mind. I wanted to see Shelda. It had been almost twenty-four hours since she'd arrived and we hadn't had ten private words together. She couldn't work for Battle around the clock. Sometime there had to be an opportunity for us to be together without interruption.

There was hell to pay upstairs. Battle was yelling the house down. There was no outside phone line in 17B. He could only talk through the switchboard, and that was being monitored. He was demanding that Jerry Dodd get the telephone company in to install an outside line at once. You and I would wait three weeks to get service from the phone company. I had a feeling Battle could get it done in a matter of minutes. Jerry kept telling him that if he wanted to make outside phone calls he could use the switchboard without being monitored — if Hardy gave his okay.

"I conduct millions of dollars' worth of very delicate business negotiations," Battle said. "I won't have some eavesdropping operator listening in, or some long-eared cop in this suite! I'll move out of this hotel if I don't get what I want, and quick!"

"That will be up to Hardy," Jerry said, not ruffling.

"Damn Hardy! Blast Hardy! Who the hell does he think he is?"

"A Homicide detective trying to solve a murder and prevent another one," Jerry said. He was as patient as a nursemaid.

I managed to interrupt long enough to say that Dr. Cobb was wanted downstairs.

"I will not be left without medical attention!" Battle said.

"I'll have Dr. Partridge, the house physician, come up," Jerry said. He turned to me. "I'll send Dr. Cobb down as soon as Partridge gets up here."

There was no sign of Shelda. I

asked if there was a chance of talking to her.

"She's gone on an errand for me," Battle said. He looked like a petulant, angry child.

Jerry went to the door with me. "He's just been in a huddle with Cobb. He doesn't need him," he said.

"Will you tell Shelda to get in touch when she gets back?"

"If that old sonofabitch will give her a chance," he said. "He's getting even with the world by keeping everybody busy."

It was a half hour before Dr. Cobb, wheezing and puffing, turned up in Chambrun's office. His emphysema, or whatever he had, made moving around really rough for him. Chambrun waved him to a comfortable armchair, but it was a good minute before the doctor was able to speak. While he struggled for breath, he managed to get out a cigarette and light it.

"Should you be smoking, Doctor?" Chambrun asked.

Cobb choked on the cigarette. Then he finally managed to say: "At my age, Mr. Chambrun, you stop caring what's good for you or not good for you. There are damn few pleasures left in life. I tell you, I could go tomorrow. Why shouldn't I enjoy today?"

"Your funeral," Chambrun said..

"A rather ghoulish comment, sir," Cobb said. "How can I help you?" A little trickle of saliva ran down his chin and he wiped it away with the back of his hand. "Could it have anything to do with the joke I made to Mr. Haskell?"

"Joke?"

"I'm afraid it was a joke," Cobb said. "I said I knew how the man in the stocking mask got into the penthouse. Is that what you're concerned about?"

"It interests me," Chambrun said.

"Puzzles have always interested me, too," Cobb said. The cigarette bobbed up and down between his lips as he spoke, ashes dribbling down his shirt front. "I had a crazy idea at the time

273

I made that remark to Mr. Haskell. Afterwards I realized that while I might have an answer as to how Stocking Mask got in the room, and how he might have chosen a time to slip away, that he couldn't have fooled George — Mr. Battle."

"Fooled him?"

Dr. Cobb was amused, but laughter made him gasp for breath. It delayed him a moment. "I — I was inclined to believe with you, Lieutenant Hardy, that the men stationed on the roof could be trusted, and that there was no way Stocking Mask could have gotten into the penthouse after we'd arrived — unless, as you thought — perhaps think — it was one of us on George's staff. Well, you trust your men; I trust ours. Of course I knew I hadn't done it, and I was completely sure that neither poor Allerton, nor Butler, nor Gaston would have done it. So someone had to have been hiding in the penthouse before we arrived — and you and I are both right. Edward Butler searched the penthouse the moment we got there. You heard him testify to that and so did I. I heard him admit he hadn't looked in the laundry hamper in the bathroom. You agreed with him that it would have been pointless. No one could hide in it, you said." The doctor shook his head and his shoulders heaved with that silent laughter of his.

"No one could have," Hardy said.

"George has such bizarre enemies," Cobb said. "He is not an ordinary man with ordinary interests, and his enemies are not ordinary. When I heard that talk about the laundry hamper, I had a wildly comical idea."

Chambrun was looking at him steadily. "Peter Potter," he said.

Cobb's eyebrows shot upward. "You mean you also thought of it, Mr. Chambrun? Now how do you like that!"

"The dwarf!" Hardy said. "He could have fitted in that damned thing!"

"He could have, but he didn't," Chambrun said. "George and you,

Dr. Cobb, and the rest of your entourage arrived at the Beaumont almost simultaneously with David Loring and the other film people. You went through the ballroom and up the service elevator to avoid them. While you were doing that Peter Potter was in the lobby with the film people. There must be over a hundred witnesses to that. So he couldn't have been hiding in the laundry hamper in advance."

"I was so amused with the idea," Cobb said, "that I couldn't resist saying I had the answer — to Mr. Haskell who was standing right beside me. Then I realized that Peter couldn't have fooled George, so I suggested to Mr. Haskell that he forget what I'd said."

"How do you mean, couldn't have fooled Battle?" Hardy asked.

"A stocking mask wouldn't disguise Peter from George," Cobb said. "He's just under four feet tall. George saw the gunman."

"You thought that Potter could have hidden in that laundry hamper,"

Chambrun said. "It must have been coupled with another thought; that Potter had a motive."

"My, my, Mr. Chambrun, it's pleasant to talk to someone whose mind isn't treacle thick. Yes, I thought Peter had a motive. Not a usual one, but a motive. I knew Peter quite well. He worked for George for about a year some time back. Was in and out of the villa fairly often. I relished his company. He has wit. He is also extremely sensitive about his deformity. He pretends to laugh at it, but it's a deep, bleeding wound in him."

"I know the story about his messenger service for George," Chambrun said.

Cobb nodded. "You and I might be annoyed at discovering we'd been acting as a dummy messenger for George," he said. "But in Peter it was a festering wound."

"Festering enough to drive him to murder five years later?"

"The whole thing was a momentary

fantasy," Cobb said. He lit a fresh cigarette from the stub of the first one. "At the time the idea amused me that he could have been hiding in the hamper and no one had bothered to look."

"You've worked for Mr. Battle for twenty years?" Hardy asked.

Cobb nodded slowly. "I have been his personal doctor for twenty years," he said, frowning.

"As we find you now, Doctor, without any outside practice?" Hardy asked.

"Yes." The doctor took a deep drag on his cigarette and choked. He had a hell of a time getting his breathing organized after that. Hardy waited for him.

"I'm guessing you're about seventy, Doctor."

"How flattering," Cobb said.

"Please tell us how you happened to give up medicine except for caring for Mr. Battle."

"It paid well," Cobb said.

"How did it begin?" Chambrun asked.

Cobb hesitated. "My practice was in the village of Cannes, in France," he said.

"But you are an American, Dr. Cobb."

"I was a medic in the army in France when the war ended," Cobb said. "I was discharged abroad and I decided to stay in France. I liked the climate in the south and I liked the people. I'd seen enough medical horros to last a man a lifetime in the army. I was satisfied to settle down to prescribing a few pills, painting a few throats, slapping a few babies on the behind. One day I got a call from the villa. George's regular doctor was on a holiday and he needed a doctor in a hurry. I went up there to see him. He was in pretty bad shape when I saw him that first time. I diagnosed it as mononucleosis. He needed rest and attention. He asked me if I'd stay there till he pulled through it. The fee he suggested was irresistible.

Chambrun smiled. "George can be irresistible when he starts talking money," he said. "I know."

Cobb nodded. "And I was lazy, and I like good food and good drink." His eyes wandered toward the sideboard. Chambrun gave me an almost imperceptible signal and I went over and poured the doctor a slug. I remembered his taste was bourbon.

"Bless you," Cobb said when I made delivery. He took a long swig. I kept thinking this old guy was hurrying the undertaker. "I stayed on with George a week — two weeks."

"And your practice?"

"It wasn't large enough for me to be badly missed." Cobb's smile was bitter. "I was the one they called when all the other doctors were too busy, or when they didn't have money to pay. Long before George was back on his feet, he asked me how I'd like a permanent job taking care of him. There's nothing basically the matter with him, you understand. His heart is good, blood pressure good, he's always afraid of getting sick, but he never does. Unlike most hypochondriacs, he doesn't have imaginary symptoms. He just wants to be prepared 'in case'. So, because I like luxury, I agreed to stay."

"Yet you were ready to prescribe sleeping pills, sedatives and that sort of thing," Chambrun said.

Cobb raised his eyes to look at the boss. "Are you suggesting that George used me as a means of supporting a narcotics habit?" he asked.

"Does he have such a habit?"

"No." Cobb finished his drink in a second long swallow. He put the glass down on the table beside his chair. "I long ago gave up trying to get him to sleep in any kind of decent stretches. Some people don't need eight-ten hours of sleep. George is one. He works twenty hours a day, taking catnaps along the way. I had a feeling that someday he would crack up. I came to understand that constant work is what keeps him going. When he dies, it will be because he has nothing to do."

"Or somebody blows him up with a greeting card," Hardy said. "After twenty years, Doctor, you must know a good deal about his private life, his friends, women."

"Women?" Cobb laughed, and choked again. "To George women are like a handsome decoration might be to you." He glanced up at the blue period Picasso on the wall. "Like that painting. He's had a string of very lovely girls acting as secretaries in my time. Not a homely one in the lot. But" — and he looked at me and grinned — "cheer up, Mr. Haskell. They are simply decorative, pleasant to look at. George's enormous energies are not channeled into sex. As for friends, Lieutenant, I have never heard George refer to anyone as a friend except Mr. Chambrun. Friends require an expenditure of time, social time. George hasn't any to give. Perhaps that's why he thinks of you as a friend, Chambrun, because you don't require anything from him, and because you live three thousand miles away."

Chambrun's face was masklike. "Maybe I have something on him," he said. "Because that's the way he operates, isn't it, Doctor? The people he trusts are people he's got something on. What does he have on you, Dr. Cobb?"

The doctor choked and struggled for breath. "I find that an offensive suggestion," he said.

"I'm trying to save a man's life, Doctor."

"You know we have reason to wonder about the people close to him," Hardy said.

The doctor was leaning forward, gasping for air. "At last Allerton is beyond suspicion," he said. "And unless I get back to my oxygen supply, you may be able to write me off, too." He struggled to his feet. "I'm sorry, gentlemen, but I'm afraid this is an emergency."

We watched him totter out of the room. He certainly wasn't faking being a very sick man.

When he had gone, Hardy stood up. "We don't seem to get anywhere fast," he said. "I'd better find out if Carlson's got anything new."

"Ask yourself a couple of questions on the way up," Chambrun said, squinting through the haze of his cigarette smoke. "Ask yourself why, when Stocking Mask missed Battle with that first shot, he didn't fire again? And ask yourself why, if the letter bomb was designed by people on the inside — Cobb, Butler, Allerton, or Gaston — the wrong person was allowed to open it?"

★ ★ ★

I didn't have time to think much about Chambrun's two questions. As Hardy was leaving, Miss Ruysdale came in to say that Shelda had just called and asked if I could meet her for

284

a drink in the Trapeze Bar. I didn't want to meet her in the Trapeze Bar, which would be crowded with people for the cocktail hour, but I went there anyway, wondering why she'd chosen this place for a get-together. There was my apartment and her room. I figured maybe she'd gotten herself tied up with the movie people and wasn't alone.

She was alone. Mr. Del Greco had put her at a little corner table. The bar was full, as I'd anticipated. Half a dozen people waved a greeting at me as I made my way between tables to Shelda. The moment I was within a yard or two of her, I knew something was wrong. Her face was chalk white. She was gripping the edge of the table, not touching the drink Del Greco had brought her. She looked up at me and I knew she'd been crying.

"Darling, what's wrong?" I asked as I slipped into the chair opposite her.

"I — I guess the whole thing has been a little too much for me, Mark," she said. "I k — keep feeling I'm responsible for what happened to Allerton."

"That's nonsense, Shelda."

"I — I'm going home," she said. "I haven't seen my family for more than a year."

"When?" I asked, feeling empty.

She glanced at her watch. "My plane leaves LaGuardia in about an hour and twenty minutes. So we haven't much time."

"Why tonight? Why not tomorrow? We haven't had a moment together. There's so much I want to talk about, Shelda."

"I can't stick it here any longer," she said, not looking at me. "Mr. Battle was very nice about it. He told me to take as long with my folks as I want to."

"That's swell," I said. "If you can get time off, you could spend it with me. Your parents can wait a few days. We have a couple of lives to decide about."

"I'm sorry, Mark. I've wired my

mother. I can't disappoint her."

I don't know why, but I was suddenly certain she wasn't telling me the truth. Whatever, it was tearing her to pieces. Her lips were quivering and she was fighting back tears.

"What is this really all about?" I asked her.

"Just what I said, Mark." She was bright and brittle. "I feel like a child not being able to take it like the rest of you. Allerton's been part of my daily life for a year. Maybe that's the reason. He was such a sweet old character."

"That's not it, Shelda. What is it? You don't have to cry over me if you've changed your mind. I gave up hoping a long time ago. I can survive one day's reversion to type."

"Please, Mark, it's not that. Will you take me to a taxi?"

"I'll go to the airport with you."

"No!" She stood up so abruptly she managed to knock over her untouched drink.

"Whatever you say." I was beginning

to feel adolescent again.

We walked down to the lobby. Mike Maggio, the bell captain, saw us and came over carrying Shelda's two bags. She was certainly going somewhere. Mike chattered about 'good flying weather' and a lot of other crap. He opened the door of a waiting taxi. Shelda started to get in, and then she turned back to me and was suddenly clinging to me. Her whole body was shaking as if she had a chill.

"Mark, please, please!" she whispered.

"What is it, baby?"

"Take care of yourself," she said. "Please take care of yourself."

And then she was in the cab and it was disappearing down Fifth Avenue. I don't mind saying I felt bewildered.

★ ★ ★

I remember I went upstairs to the second floor to my own office after Shelda had split down the Avenue, headed for her parents' home in

Kansas. I had their address and phone number stashed away in my office and I thought I'd copy it down so that I could call her later — much later.

I hadn't been at my desk since noon the day before. My secretary had gone home, but she had left a stack of mail for me and some notations about urgent phone calls. The chairman for a political dinner was screaming for an interview with Mr. Amato, our banquet manager. A famous couturier wanted to know when they could have a full dress rehearsal, with models, for an exhibition of his new line which was supposed to take place in the ballroom next week. The P.R. man for a famous Hollywood star wanted to buy me lunch and talk about his client who was due to check in at the Beaumont next Thursday. My secretary had handled what she could, but there were a dozen personal calls I should have answered. They'd all have to wait till tomorrow, I told myself.

I heard the outer door of my office

open and close. I'd neglected to lock it when I came in, and I looked up to see Maxie Zorn, the movie tycoon, standing in the inner office door.

"Thank God there's somebody alive in this place," he said. "Can I come in?"

I waved him to a chair beside my desk.

"I can't get in touch with anyone," he said. "Switchboard won't put me through to Battle. What in Christ's world is going on around here, Haskell?"

"Murder and attempted murder," I said. "The cops get awfully touchy about that, and Mr. Chambrun is even worse when it happens in his hotel."

"Can you tell me what the hell is going on?"

"Someone sent Battle an exploding letter," I said. "It got the valet by mistake. The cops and the hotel have Battle covered like a tent. That's why you can't get to him."

"Do you have any idea what's going on in my life?" Maxie asked. He sounded anguished.

"You're waiting for seven million bucks to get close enough for you to grab," I said. "It must be nerve-racking."

"I'm going to lose a star if I don't get answers quick," Maxie said. "David Loring always has more offers than he can handle. He's waited for a final answer from me about as long as he can and will. If I lose him, the whole thing falls apart. A picture with David in it makes money even if it's lousy. Without him — !" He made a helpless gesture with nervous hands.

"About the best I can do is offer you a drink," I said. I wondered if it would be a kindness to tell him that I knew Battle was just playing games with him in order to prevent Cleaves' novel from being filmed.

"I don't drink," Maxie said. "Can you get a message to Battle for me?"

"I could try," I said.

"It's simple enough," he said. "Let him know that if I don't have an answer by after breakfast tomorrow, we'll lose David. And what about your girl friend? Is she going to play ball or not?"

"She's on her way to Kansas," I said.

"I don't care where she is," Maxie said. "We wouldn't get to film her sequence for months. But will she do it?"

I felt sorry for him. "I don't think she will, Maxie, and I don't think Battle cares. He was just trying to do her a favor, and if she doesn't want it, that isn't going to stand in your way. What he wants, I gather, is control of the script."

"Why?" Maxie wailed. "He's not a writer! He mentioned this to me a while back and I thought Cleaves was going to have apoplexy. It's no secret Cleaves hates Battle's guts. Something about his father got killed in the big war by friends of Battle's. Cleaves has final say-so on the script. That's in my contract with him."

"Maybe what Battle wants wouldn't be objectionable to Cleaves," I said.

"Anything Battle wants would be objectionable to Cleaves. He's tried to find other money for me because he didn't want Battle involved — right from the beginning. Somehow or other Battle's got other doors shut on us."

"Maybe he can't keep 'em shut forever," I said.

"Long enough so I lose David," Maxie said. "The people who put up money put it up for the star, not for the story. Try and get through to Battle for me, will you, Haskell? I know you better than to offer you bread. But I might be able to do you a return favor sometime. You might not want to spend the rest of your life in this hotel. You might make it big doing P.R. work in films."

"I'll try to get to him because I feel sorry for you. What's going on around here shouldn't happen to a dog," I said.

My phone rang and I picked it up.

It was Miss Ruysdale.

"Glad I found you, Mark," she said. "Mr. Chambrun wants you."

"What's up?" I asked.

"Dr. Cobb," she said.

"What about him?"

"He's dead, Mark."

"God. Less than an hour ago — ! How did it happen?"

"He seems simply to have stopped breathing," Ruysdale said.

4

WHEN you have been surrounded by violence as we had for the last twenty-four hours, a natural death seemed like adding insult to injury. George Battle put it in a rather apt way.

"Even God seems to be against me," he said. "In the midst of all this hell I lose an old and trusted friend."

There wasn't much to the story I heard when I joined Chambrun up in 17B, Battle's suite. Dr. Cobb, it seemed, had returned from his visit to Chambrun's office in pretty bad shape. Doc Partridge, our house physician, had been there when he got back. Jerry Dodd had produced the doc to stand by Battle while Cobb was out of the suite. Doc is old, cantankerous, with bushy black eyebrows contrasting with his silvery hair.

"Damned old fool," he said to Chambrun and the rest of us. Hardy was there, too. The Lieutenant had to be certain he didn't have another homicide on his hands. "He had no business being up and around. Do an autopsy on him and you'll find he doesn't have anything but torn rags for lungs. But he went on smoking and drinking and trying to live a normal life."

"Perhaps that was the best way to see it through," Chambrun said.

"And shorten the process," Doc Partridge said. "When he got back here, I didn't think he'd make it to his room. Strangling, he was; gasping for breath. I figured if he didn't get to his oxygen supply in a hurry, he'd had it. I helped him into his room and got him down on the bed and got the oxygen cylinder where he could use it, the mask over his nose and mouth. He waved a sort of thanks at me and I left him. Then he lifted the mask off his face and managed to say something about 'sleeves'. I didn't get it, but I went back to him. He was sucking in oxygen from the tank. He knew how bad it was, he was a doctor."

Chambrun was frowning. "What did he mean, 'sleeves'?"

"I couldn't figure it," Doc said. "I'd helped him off with his suit jacket. I looked at his shirt sleeves. They were fairly tight around his wrists, so I unbuttoned them. They could have caused him some discomfort. He shook his head as if he was trying to tell me that wasn't it, but he was too busy trying to breath to go any further with it."

"Wasn't there anything you could do to help him, Doc?"

"Oxygen was the only thing that would help him," Doc said. "Best thing was to leave him quietly alone with it. So I came back out here and reported the state of things to Mr. Battle. Half an hour later I went back into the bedroom to see how he was doing. He was gone. Dead."

"Shouldn't you have stayed with him?" Chambrun asked.

"No reason to. He knew exactly how to handle things. Lie perfectly still and get some oxygen down into what was left of his lungs."

"Why didn't it work?"

Doc shrugged. "You come to the end of a dead-end street. There comes a last time when nothing works."

Battle was huddled in a big armchair, looking woebegone. Butler, the bodyguard, and Gaston, the chef, were hovering in the background.

"I was wrong to come here, Pierre," Battle said. "My impulse is to arrange to head back for home tonight, at once. But to go back to the villa without Allerton — without Cobb — "

"I'd like to have a look at him," Chambrun said to Doc, as if he hadn't heard Battle.

Partridge led the way into the bedroom. What was left of Dr. Cobb wasn't a pleasant sight. He'd worn dentures and he'd taken them out and put them on the bedside table. His jaw, slack, hung open, revealing an ugly black hole. The oxygen tank and mask were on a chair several feet away from the bed. Partridge saw Chambrun looking at them.

"I put them there," he said. "The mask was on his face and the cylinder lying beside him on the bed when I found him."

Chambrun went over and picked up the cylinder. I saw his frown deepen.

"Poor bastard," he said. "The damned thing is empty."

"Impossible!" Doc said.

Chambrun turned. "What do you mean, 'impossible'? See for yourself." He held out the cylinder to Doc.

Partridge took it, examined it. "You're right, but it's still impossible."

"Why?"

"It was brand-new," Doc said. "I got it for him late this afternoon. You don't carry extras around in your luggage. Too bulky. He called my office and asked me to get him a fresh one.

There's a regular supply service for them and I had this one delivered."

"How do you know it was that one?"

"Tag on it. Name of the supplier on it. My supplier. I brought this up to him myself. He used it just before he went down to see you. It was full."

"Maybe he forgot to turn it off."

"When your life depends on something, you don't forget simple routines," Partridge said.

"Maybe the cylinder is faulty — has a leak in it."

"Be a damn good idea to find out," Doc said. "Because if it isn't — "

"Just what I was thinking, Doc," Chambrun said. "You take charge of it, Doc. Get someone here to check it out." He glanced toward the door to the living room. "For now, just between us. Right?"

Doc took the cylinder and went out. Chambrun and Hardy and I stood looking down at the dead Cobb.

"You trying to make something out

of nothing?" Hardy asked.

"I hope so," Chambrun said. He turned to me. "I haven't seen Shelda around."

"She's gone," I said.

"Gone?"

"Home. To beautiful downtown Topeka, Kansas," I said.

"What are you talking about?"

"Her family," I said. "She hasn't seen them for more than a year. This all got a little too rough for her. Battle gave her some free time, so she took off."

"When?" Chambrun sounded sharper than the subject required.

I glanced at my watch. "Her plane must have left LaGuardia sometime in the last half hour," I said.

"You know the flight number?"

"No."

"Find out."

"How?"

"The chances are ten to one she made her reservation through the travel service downstairs. Find out what it is."

"Why are you so interested? I don't get it," I said.

"That's because you are an idiot," Chambrun said, and sounded like he meant it. "Just what did she tell you? You did see her?"

"Sure I saw her. In the Trapeze. She was pretty badly shaken up. She felt somehow responsible for what happened to Allerton. If he hadn't taken the letters in for her — Nonsense, of course. So she wanted to get out."

His eyes were those narrowed slits that told of anger. "Find out the number of her flight if you can," he said. "And then check at the airport to see if she actually took it."

"Of course she took it," I said.

"Listen," Chambrun said. "That girl is in love with you. She wouldn't take off to see her family when you haven't had ten minutes together. She wouldn't be shaken up by what's happened. She has the guts of a burglar. You don't know your own woman. Just find out about the flight and if she took it. If

302

she didn't, God help her."

"Would you mind telling me what you're hinting at?" I asked, feeling a knot tightening in my stomach.

"I'm not hinting," he said. "I'm telling you she may be in serious trouble. There isn't time to draw you pictures. Find out what we have to know, and don't stop on the way to pass the time of day with anyone."

It wasn't like him to be mysterious. His concern for Shelda just didn't make any sense. Yet he always made sense. I tried to remember everything she'd said, exactly how she'd looked. There wasn't anything, except that she had certainly cracked up.

Chambrun was right about the travel service. They had made the reservation for Shelda. Flight 074 to Topeka, leaving LaGuardia at 7:10 P.M. I called the airport. Shelda hadn't picked up the reservation. I felt a sudden chill running along my spine as I headed back upstairs to find Chambrun.

He and Hardy had left 17B when

I got there. Jerry Dodd, who was still standing guard, didn't know where they'd gone.

"Battle has given orders for his yachts to be ready to take him back to France by midnight," Jerry said. "Hardy has told him he couldn't go while he was needed here as a material witness. Would you believe there has been a direct call to the State Department and that Hardy has been advised not to be sticky?"

"Our Mr. Battle has friends in high places," I said. "Would you have any idea what's bugging Chambrun about Shelda?"

He grinned at me. "Shelda who?" he said.

I wasn't in the mood for jokes, but I didn't have the chance to tell Jerry so because Battle came out of the bedroom.

"I'm glad I have a chance to talk to you, Haskell," he said. He walked over to the big armchair and sat down. Almost instantly Gaston, the chef, appeared carrying a tray with two cups and a pot of tea. He went through the same routine I'd seen Allerton handle up in the penthouse. He poured tea into both cups, took one himself, tasted, waited a moment till it cooled a little, drank more heartily. Then he handed the second cup to Battle.

"Thank you, Gaston," Battle said. He sipped his tea with apparent relish. Then he remembered me. "I know you have done what you can, Haskell, to keep the buzzards of the press off my back. I appreciate your efforts."

"My job," I said.

"There will be a little more to it," he said. "In spite of the objections of your police lieutenant I will be setting out for the marina where my yachts are anchored a little after eleven o'clock. It's going to be very difficult to get out of the hotel without being swamped by those reporters, in spite of what Pierre and his people can do."

"They're hungry to talk to you,"

I said. I wanted out. I wanted to find Chambrun with my news about Shelda.

"I would like you to call a formal press conference for eleven o'clock in one of your special reception rooms downstairs," Battle said. "I will give you a statement for them."

"And while I'm talking to them, you slip out of the hotel," I said.

He smiled that smile that must have been so attractive years ago. "Exactly right," he said.

"And then I had better look for a job in another field," I said. "The minute I play tricks on the reporters my usefulness as a public relations man for the hotel is finished."

"Your first loyalty is to Pierre," he said. "I'm sure he will approve."

"When he says so, I'll arrange it," I said.

The phone rang and Jerry answered it. "For you," he said to me. "Message for you. The boss wants you in his office."

"Then you can arrange things with Pierre at once," Battle said, "and let the press know that you'll have a statement from me for them at eleven o'clock."

"If Mr. Chambrun says so."

Battle's smile widened. "You can count on it that he will."

★ ★ ★

Chambrun, Hardy, and Miss Ruysdale were in the boss's office when I got there. I sensed a kind of special tension between them that I didn't understand. Chambrun turned on me, sounding angry.

"I told you not to hang around talking to people," he said.

"Not people," I said. "The Great Man himself. In a way I work for him, you know."

"You work for me," Chambrun said, "and don't forget it, Mark. What did George want?"

"I'm to call a fake press conference

while he and his army slip out of the hotel and head for his yacht, or yachts. You, he says, will authorize it."

Chambrun and Hardy exchanged glances.

"For what time?" Chambrun asked.

"Eleven o'clock, on the button."

The corner of Chambrun's mouth twitched. "I authorize it," he said. He turned to Miss Ruysdale. "Will you get word to the reporters downstairs that Mark will have a statement for them at eleven? In the Crystal Dining Room." Ruysdale took off for her office and Chambrun was back at me. "Shelda?" he asked.

"She didn't make the plane or didn't take it," I said. "The reservation was made by our people, but she didn't pick it up."

"Jesus!" Hardy said, under his breath.

Something exploded inside me. "Will you tell me what this Shelda business is about?" I shouted at Chambrun. "Do you have to treat me like some goddam retarded child?"

I might as well not have spoken. "Did the taxi Shelda took come out of the line waiting in front of the hotel, or did you flag down a cruiser?" Chambrun asked.

"It came out of the line — I think," I said. "Mike Maggio had her bags and the cab slid up to us the minute he appeared."

"I don't suppose you recognized the driver?" He reached out and picked up his house phone on the desk. "Get Mike Maggio, but quick," he said. Then back to me. "I don't suppose you did anything intelligent like taking down his license number?"

"I've had just about enough of this," I shouted at him again. "Why the hell should I take down his license number? What is this, Mr. Chambrun? So help me God, I — "

He made an impatient silencing gesture. He spoke into the phone. "Mike? You put Shelda Mason into a cab an hour or so ago. Yes. Yes, I know Mark was with you. Was the driver one of the regular ones in the line? You know him? Good boy. Mike, I've got to find that guy just as fast as it can possibly be done. Tell him there's a hundred dollar bill in it for him if he makes it here by ten forty-five. Thanks, Mike. It's really important." Chambrun put down the phone and he looked, suddenly, very tired. "I'm sorry, Mark," he said, all the edge gone off his voice. "I had to get you to answer questions quickly, yes or no. I'm not angry at you. I'm angry at myself for having been so stupidly slow!"

"About Shelda," I said, trying to hold onto myself.

"I told you, Mark, you don't know her as well as you should. She doesn't crack up in crisis. Try to remember back to the time she worked here and was tested. I think Shelda heard something, found out something. Before she could get to us with it, she was caught."

"Caught? By whom?"

"I'm not dead sure," Chambrun said.

"But whoever it was scared her into leaving the hotel."

"But she was perfectly free to go or not," I said.

"She was free to tell you she was going home to her parents," Chambrun said, "which we now know she hasn't done."

"We were alone in the Trapeze," I said. "She could have told me."

"I think not," Chambrun said. "You wouldn't have let her go."

"She wouldn't scare that easily," I said. "You've said so yourself."

"She might," Chambrun said. "If the threat was aimed at someone else, she might. You, Mark. She does what she's told to do or you get it. The girl loves you, Mark. She'd play any kind of game to keep you out of danger. I could kick myself around the block because I figured some kind of a play of this sort. I expected it to come later. I thought it might be Ruysdale they'd aim at. Whatever Shelda stumbled on made them move faster than I think they'd planned."

"You keep saying 'they'," I said.

"Figure of speech," Chambrun said. "Surely you must see there's been more than one body involved in this from the start. The man in the stocking mask who fired at George; the man in the stocking mask who kidnaped me; the man who delivered the letters; the man who emptied Dr. Cobb's oxygen cylinder so that he died for want of it."

"You know that?"

Chambrun nodded. "The cylinder wasn't faulty. Someone emptied it while Cobb was down here talking to us."

"No fingerprints on it except Cobb's, Doc Partridge's, and Mr. Chambrun's," Hardy said, answering a question before I could ask it.

"Is that what Shelda found out? She caught someone emptying the cylinder?" I asked.

"It's possible," Chambrun said. "Or she overheard a conversation. Or she came across something in her notes that told her something."

"It had to be somebody up in Seventeen B," I said. "Butler? Gaston? Battle himself?"

Chambrun hesitated, taking time to light a cigarette. "There have been two forces operating here from the start, Mark. George Battle broke the habits of two decades to come here to nail down Richard Cleaves. He had to stop that film being made, and I know why now. I've had a brief look at the novel and the script. There were at least two other people who knew why. Allerton and Dr. Cobb."

"Both dead!"

"Yes, Mark, but I'm still alive." I think he meant to go on, but Ruysdale appeared in the doorway.

"The reporters have been alerted," she said. "And your two guests are here."

"Have them brought in. And take notes, Ruysdale."

Ruysdale stepped aside and Richard

Cleaves and Peter Potter came into the office, accompanied by two of Hardy's plainclothes men. The little dwarf was smiling his bright smile. He gestured toward the two cops.

"Are we being protected, or are you being protected, Chambrun?" he asked. He perched on the arm of a chair, his short legs dangling. Cleaves stood very straight and still, expressionless behind the black glasses.

"There are a great many things I'd like to say to you two," Chambrun said, moving around behind his desk, "but I only have time for one of them. You are a pair of cold-blooded liars."

Potter giggled. "You've read the script," he said.

Cleaves stood still as a statue.

"I've glanced at the script," Chambrun said. "May I remind you that my association with George Battle goes back more than twenty years. I go farther back than our two dead friends, Allerton and Cobb."

That jarred Cleaves. "Dr. Cobb is dead?"

"Expired from lack of oxygen," Chambrun said. "Just before he died, he tried to ask for you."

I didn't remember any such thing and I gave Chambrun a puzzled look.

"Doc Partridge thought he said something about 'sleeves'," Chambrun said. "Of course what he said was 'Cleaves'! He wanted to warn you, Mr. Cleaves, or get your help. The lack of oxygen, by the way, was a practical fact. Somebody emptied his cylinder. Had someone guessed that Cobb was collaborating with you, Cleaves?"

"That's a shot in the dark," Cleaves said in his flat, hard voice.

"Look here, Mr. Cleaves, I suspect your novel, read at leisure, would be quite fascinating. But George Battle referred to the first fifty pages as being of concern to him. I found there the story of an assassination, apparently arranged by political enemies. In the script, Mr. Cleaves, you have changed your motives somewhat. In the script your mastermind is someone interested in a fabulous oil contract. In your script a second man is killed trying to protect the victim. But I don't have to tell you about your changes. No wonder George Battle wants it stopped. Twenty-two years ago he engineered just such a coup. And twenty-two years ago, Cleaves, the real victim's trusted bodyguard — you made him a brother in your story — wasn't on hand to protect him. He was in the hay with a beautiful girl planted by the mastermind. That isn't in your novel."

"It's just a sex scene to make the film more salable," Potter said.

"Nonsense. It's a factual detail that was part of the real life story. Somebody fed you these details, Cleaves. You were happy to use them because your source made it clear to you that when the film appeared George Battle would be revealed to enemies who would almost certainly find a way to kill him. Was it

Cobb, or Allerton, or both? They had been with him long enough to know or guess at the true story. Or was it you, Potter? Had Cobb, in some drunken moment while you were working for George, let it slip?"

"A complete pipe dream, Mr. Chambrun," Potter said.

"I ask you one more question, and God help you if you don't answer it honestly, Cleaves. Have you already tipped off the people who would want to kill Battle? You have dreamed for a lifetime of getting revenge. This would be an ideal way, leaving you completely innocent."

Cleaves stood straight and silent.

"There isn't time for games," Chambrun said. "If I've made a right guess, then you know that Shelda Mason is in mortal danger, and I promise you that if anything happens to her I will personally see to it that you go just as colorfully as your father went."

"You sonofabitch," Cleaves said tonelessly.

"Last chance for some truth," Chambrun said.

A little trickle of sweat ran down Cleaves' cheek. "I think you just told me that Cobb was murdered," he said.

"That's what I told you."

"And someone is threatening the Mason girl?"

"Yes."

Potter laughed. "Uncle George Battle is an original. He won't stop at anything, will he?"

"I'm sick of games and I haven't got time for them," Chambrun said. "Someone took a shot at George; someone tried to kill him with a letter bomb; I, his friend, was kidnaped and held for ransom; his two most trusted employees are dead. I suggest Dr. Cobb revealed these new facts to you, Cleaves, after he'd read your book. I suggest you took them, happily, added them to the film script, and passed along what you knew to people who were ready and willing to wipe him out when they heard the truth."

Cleaves shook his head slowly. "You're half right," he said. "Only half right, Mr. Chambrun."

"Which half?"

Cleaves took a deep breath and let it out slowly. "My book was pure invention," he said. "Not too many suspense novels reach the best seller lists. Mine did. Maxie Zorn made me an immediate offer for it — an extremely good deal contingent upon his getting the financing for it."

"In other words, he took an option on it?"

"Yes. A generous option. Getting financing didn't seem to be a difficult matter, particularly after Maxie got David Loring to agree to star in it. It happened almost at once. George Battle offered to put up the money under certain conditions. We were to go to France to discuss those conditions.

"You can imagine my state of mind. Maxie knew nothing about my past, my personal feelings about George Battle. I didn't want Battle involved, but, on the other hand, I was curious. I wondered if Battle knew who I was. For fifteen years I'd been trying to get to him, and now I was invited to his house, for God sake. So we flew to France and went to the villa in Cannes.

"The beginning of that session was reasonable enough. Battle would put up the money, seven million dollars, provided he was satisfied with the film script. He wanted at least a scene-by-scene outline of what the film would be. And he wanted the right to disapprove anything he didn't like."

"Not unreasonable if you're putting up seven million dollars," Chambrun said.

"Perhaps not. But I wasn't having any. George Battle, my enemy, wasn't going to control my work. I said so, and I told him who I was — Richard St. Germaine. He really blew his stack on that. Ordered me out of the house. Told me I would never be readmitted. I left, supposing the deal was off, satisfied that I'd jarred him a little. Maxie, not understanding, stayed on to plead with him. To my surprise, Battle didn't back away. His dislike of me, he told Maxie, was personal. He would still put up the money if he got an outline of the script. Maxie caught up with me at the hotel in town where we were staying. He asked me to do an outline. I told him to go to hell. I went out on the town to get thoroughly drunk. That's when I met Dr. Cobb. I'd seen him, briefly, at the villa. I didn't realize, at first, that he'd come looking for me. I'll try to boil down his story."

Chambrun glanced at his watch. "Please," he said.

"Battle doesn't trust people," Cleaves said. "Dr. Cobb, Allerton, Butler, Gaston, other people who have worked for him over the years, weren't just bought with big salaries and nice treatment. Battle had something on each of them, something big. If any one of them betrayed him, if anything happened to Battle, they would all be facing prison, the gallows, or whatever the maximum is in France. The guillotine? Nice little arrangement. Not only was each one of them threatened, but each one of them was watching the other, because betrayal by one meant the works for all of them.

"Cobb had read my book. He'd been astonished to see how closely, in many ways, it paralleled an incident in Battle's life. He told me the reason Battle wanted in was that he wanted to be sure nothing was added that would be a complete giveaway. Having found out who I was, Battle suspected I might know more than was in the book, that I would add this more to the film, and that Middle East terrorists who saw it would recognize the truth and find a way to get him. Of course I didn't know anything more. I had invented a plot. It happened to match something real in some respects. That much I could have gotten out of old newspaper clippings. Cobb offered to give me other facts that would blow Battle sky-high."

"He was risking his own hide," Chambrun said. "How much did he ask you to pay for these facts?"

"Not a penny," Cleaves said. "You see, Mr. Chambrun, Cobb was a doctor. He knew exactly what his own physical condition was. He knew he had a very limited time left on this earth. He decided that a last pleasure for him would be to see Battle on the hook, hopefully eliminated. He guessed that would also give me pleasure. And so he talked, and he told me things, and I went back to the hotel and told Maxie I'd do an outline. I did. It went back to Battle in three or four days. Then he knew that I knew, and that the film mustn't be done that way at any cost. He stalled, he made new conditions — apparently unimportant ones like insisting Miss Mason should play the girl in the nude scene. He also spread the word, and Maxie found other sources of money shut off. The real condition was, of course, that he had editorial control of the script. The new material would have to be out, but he didn't say that. Not yet. I knew, of course. Finally he announced that he would come to New York to close the deal. I got pleasure out of watching him wriggle, Chambrun. There was something macabre about the final arrangements. We were all to be here at the Beaumont. Battle and you under the same roof."

Chambrun's smile was grim. "You found that tempting?"

"Not really. You see I had Battle by the short hairs."

"Didn't it occur to you that you were in danger? If something happened to you here in New York, no one would tie it into George."

"Wrong," Cleaves said. "A copy of that script you read is in my lawyer's safe. If anything happens to me, he'll know how to use it. That's the half of your guess that's right, Chambrun. The other half? I've never contacted the people who will be interested in the script, Battle's enemies. I wouldn't know how to contact them. Neither did Cobb. The produced film was to be our way of telling them. According to Cobb, they had an army of dedicated assassins at their disposal."

"An elaborate and very neat murder plan," Chambrun said.

"But I doubt provable in court," Cleaves said.

"Can you be sure Cobb hadn't given these assassins advance notice?"

"What can you be sure of in this world? He told me he hadn't, didn't know how to."

Chambrun turned his eyes, the eyes of a hanging judge, on Potter. "But you would know how, wouldn't you, Potter? You were a secret messenger. You knew many of the ins and outs of George's functioning. You probably knew much of the story Cobb told Cleaves. How was it? Didn't you want to wait for the film? You set George and his people up, here in my hotel, as a target for his would-be killers. You even told them how I could be used to raise money for them. Is that how it was?"

Potter grinned. "I wish I'd thought of it," he said.

Chambrun glanced at his watch again. "In just half an hour Battle is leaving for home. In fifteen minutes you'll be holding your press conference, Mark. Is it arranged for?" He glanced at Miss Ruysdale.

"In the Crystal Dining Room," she said.

"I'm supposed to get a statement from Battle for the press," I said.

"I'll go with you," Chambrun said, giving me an odd smile. "As for you two, Cleaves and Potter, the lieutenant should place you under arrest as material witnesses. If anything happens to George Battle before he gets out of Hardy's jurisdiction, you would both be charged with conspiracy to commit a very fancy homicide."

Potter's smile had frozen a little.

"You disappoint me, Mr. Chambrun," he said. "After all these years of dealing with George Battle you seem to overlook the fact that nothing that happens in his life is ever what it appears to be. If I saw him dead, I wouldn't believe it."

★ ★ ★

Mike Maggio was waiting in Miss Ruysdale's office when Chambrun and Hardy and I went out there. With him was a little man with a taxi driver's license pinned to his cap.

"Fred Tenaccio," Mike said. "He's the driver you wanted, Mr. Chambrun. He remembers driving Shelda — Miss Mason."

"Where to?" Chambrun asked.

"LaGuardia," the little man said. "That's where she told me to go, that's where I took her. Good tipper, that doll."

"Were you late? Traffic problems?"

"Easy rolling," the driver said. "She

said she had to catch a seven-ten plane. We were there twenty minutes to. No problem."

"Then why didn't she take the plane?" I asked Chambrun.

"She wasn't allowed to," he said.

"Maybe I ought to go out there," I said. "Maybe she was taken ill. She could be in the airport hospital."

"No chance," Chambrun said. "Ruysdale, give Mr. Tenaccio a hundred dollars, please."

"Gee, Mr. Chambrun, just for answering two questions?" Tenaccio said. "You don't owe me nothing. Glad to be useful."

"Never question your luck, Mr. Tenaccio," Chambrun said. He turned to Hardy. "You'll cover the point I suggested?"

"On my way," Hardy said.

I didn't ask what the 'point' was. There was a heavy iron lump in my stomach. Shelda had been wide open for some kind of attack, if I read Chambrun correctly. How bad could it be? She'd been at the airport, with hundreds of people all around. I wanted to call out there; find out from someone if anything unusual had happened between twenty of seven and seven-ten. Chambrun didn't seem concerned. We went out into the hall and took an elevator to the seventeenth floor.

In 17B there were all the signs of eminent departure. Luggage was stacked near the door. Butler and Gaston were dressed for travel. George Battle was sitting on the couch, his big black overcoat and floppy black hat resting beside him. And Maxie Zorn was there, looking very happy.

"Mr. Zorn and I have come to an agreement about the film," Battle said.

"The author is agreeable?" Chambrun asked.

"Every man has his price," Battle said. "The author will be agreeable. Have you arranged for the press meeting, Mr. Haskell?"

"Yes, sir," I said.

"I'll handle that for you, George,"

Chambrun said. "I can keep them busy for as long as is necessary. Your two Cadillacs will be at a side entrance at exactly eleven-ten. Jerry, you'll take Mr. Battle down on the service elevator and out the way we discussed."

"Right," Jerry Dodd said.

"You won't have to go through the lobby, George," Chambrun said. "No chance of any encounters. Jerry will ride shotgun along with Butler until you reach your boat. After that you're on your own. But then you have your own little army on the yacht, don't you? So no problem then."

"No problem at all," Battle said. "Thank you for everything, Pierre. God knows I wish I hadn't brought you so much trouble." He stood up and held out his hand to Chambrun.

"You're not concerned with whether we catch our murderer, George?" Chambrun asked.

"I'm concerned," Battle said, "but I prefer to be concerned at a safe distance."

Chambrun shook the outstretched hand and then glanced at his watch. "I'd better get down to the gentlemen of the press," he said. "Jerry, get this caravan started at exactly eleven."

"Right," Jerry said.

"Good-by, George."

"Good-by, Pierre. I trust it won't take too long to get your penthouse livable again."

"I'll manage, George," Chambrun said. "It's a big hotel."

We left. Out in the hall I pressured him as we waited for an elevator. "Don't we do anything about Shelda?" I asked.

He turned and put a hand on my shoulder. "Try to trust me, Mark," he said. "I don't really know why you should, because I've been so slow, so stupid. But let me assure you that if it is possible to do anything for Shelda, it's being done."

"There must be something I can do," I said. I felt desperate. "I don't think you know what it's like, not knowing, not doing anything to help her."

"I think I know," he said. "But if I'm right, Mark, Shelda's in this trouble because she's trying to protect you. The best thing you can do for her is to stay out of trouble."

"Protect me from whom?" I asked.

"Someone she knows is a killer," Chambrun said.

★ ★ ★

The Crystal Dining Room is on the lobby level, its entrance on the south side of the lobby, adjoining the Blue Lagoon, the Beaumont's night club. When Chambrun and I arrived there, the place was jammed with reporters and cameramen. There was even a TV camera set up. The boys and girls seemed delighted to see someone a little more colorful than Mark Haskell. Chambrun had always been good copy.

He walked to the far end of the room where there was a small raised platform. For banquets this platform was used for a speaker's table. A speaker system was set up there. Miss Ruysdale had left nothing undone. Chambrun mounted the platform and held up his hands for silence. I looked at my watch. We were two or three minutes later starting than we had promised.

"Ladies and gentlemen," Chambrun said, "may I have your attention, please. I'm going to give you a very complete and detailed story of what's been going on in this hotel for the last thirty hours. If I'm to do that, I would like to ask that you do not interrupt me with questions until I've come to the end. It's not a simple story, and if you interrupt with questions before I tell it all, you'll be frustrated by the confusion that will result. If I seem to be withholding something, or not explaining it to your satisfaction, bear with me. When I've finished, I promise not to cut the question period short. Satisfactory?"

There was a chorus of approval.

"So the beginning was yesterday a little after five o'clock. Mr. George

Battle arrived here at the hotel, accompanied by his personal staff, which consisted of a man named Allerton, his valet; a Dr. Cobb, who was his personal physician; Edward Butler, who is his bodyguard; a man called Gaston, who is his personal chef; and his secretary, Shelda Mason, who is a former employee here at the Beaumont. You don't need a dossier on Mr. Battle. It's in all your morgue files. You do know that he is the owner of this hotel, and an old associate of mine, dating back to long before I held my present job.

"It had been arranged that Mr. Battle and his staff should stay in a penthouse on the roof which belongs to me. I moved, in advance, into other quarters. Mr. Battle has been frequently described as an eccentric; his precautions in travel, his food taster, his special bodyguard and special doctor, what is literally an armed fortress that he lives in France. People classify this as neurosis, hypochondria, God knows what else. Let me assure you that Mr. Battle's fear of being attacked, personally, is entirely legitimate. No man who wields his kind of power is ever safe from the revenge of small men and counterattacks from other powerful groups. It was not, therefore, simply to satisfy a neurotic whim that we took extraordinary precautions to protect the penthouse from approach from outside. The one elevator that goes to the roof had one of our security men stationed on it along with an operator. We had three men patrolling the roof outside the penthouse. Inside was Edward Butler, Mr. Battle's bodyguard, armed and on the alert. There is a fire stair exit from the penthouse vestibule. It was locked on the inside. No way to get in without being seen and stopped.

"Mr. Battle went to bed about nine o'clock. He was tired from his trip. About ten he woke, certain that someone was in his room. He assumed it was either Dr. Cobb or Allerton, his valet. He switched on the bedside lamp and found himself facing a man wearing a stocking mask, who was pointing a gun at him. The man fired, the bullet entering the headboard of the bed about six inches from Mr. Battle's forehead. The man in the mask then cried out and ran away through the bathroom.

"Now let me tell you what the setup was inside the penthouse. Butler, the bodyguard, was sitting in a chair, backed up against the door of the bedroom. He was armed and awake. He had previously searched the apartment and knew there was no one in the penthouse except the people I've mentioned — excluding Miss Mason, who was quartered elsewhere. Butler could see not only the front door but down a corridor to the other bedrooms and the bathroom I've mentioned. He swears that no one went into the bedroom. The minute he heard the shot, he pushed aside his chair and ran into the bedroom. Mr. Battle was huddled in bed, pointing to the bathroom, through which the man in the mask had escaped. Now the man in the mask could have gotten away without being seen by Butler. It's just possible he could have gotten out on the roof. Our men out there had also heard the shot and were rushing in to find out what had happened. The man in the mask could have gotten out, but at this moment, feeling certain that nobody goofed, neither I nor the police are able to tell you how he got in."

There was a rumble from the news people, but Chambrun held up his hand. "Remember, questions later." He smiled at them. "Enter the police and the District Attorney's office. Mr. Battle was in shock, and Dr. Cobb reported he had given him a sedative that would knock him out for several hours — at least until morning. He couldn't be questioned. I went down to my office. About eleven o'clock I received a phone call — through my secretary — saying that Mr. Kranepool, the assistant D.A., wanted me back in the penthouse. I left my office and found myself confronted in the corridor by an armed man wearing a stocking mask. At gun point I was taken out of the hotel to an address about three blocks from here."

The rumble started again. This was news.

"I was placed in a chair, my wrists handcuffed behind me, adhesive tape placed over my mouth, and left alone. I didn't know then what I know now, of course. There was a phone call to the penthouse demanding ransom — one hundred thousand dollars. Mr. Battle arranged for it. Mark Haskell was designated by the kidnaper to deliver it. He did, and I was released. That was a little after ten this morning.

"I came back to the hotel and while I was trying to get cleaned up and into fresh clothes, mail was delivered to the penthouse for Mr. Battle. This mail was delivered to a detective on the elevator by a man he assumed was a hotel employee. The elevator operator assumed he was a detective. The detective handed the mail to Lieutenant Hardy in the penthouse. There were half a dozen business letters and what looked like a greeting card. Allerton, the valet, took the mail into the bedroom. Mr. Battle was in the bathroom. Allerton called to him and told him there was mail, and evidently a birthday card. It is Mr. Battle's birthday. Mr. Battle told Allerton to open the card. He did, and the place blew up, killing Allerton, injuring Butler, who was in the room, and Mr. Battle, who was cut by flying glass in the bathroom.

"That, gentlemen and ladies, was all for a while. Then, late this afternoon, Dr. Cobb was found dead in his room. You understand we had been forced to move Mr. Battle to another suite because of the bomb damage. Dr. Cobb suffered from an acute emphysema and his death seemed to be from natural causes, except that we discovered that the oxygen cylinder which might have saved his life had been emptied by someone.

"That is it, ladies and gentlemen. I should add that, not surprisingly, Mr. Battle doesn't feel very safe here and he is already on his way back to France." There were groans from the press. Chambrun smiled at them. "Any questions?"

That brought a laugh, and a dozen hands were raised. My friend from the *News* was in there first, as usual.

"You say you can't tell us how the masked man got into the penthouse. You must have a theory."

"I have a theory," Chambrun said. "Hardy had a theory. He thought it must be someone already in — Cobb, Allerton, Butler, Gaston. They were all searched, literally down to their skins, for the gun, the mask, any proof of that theory. Nothing."

"But you said Butler had a gun?"

"Not the one that fired the shot into the headboard," Chambrun said. "Wrong caliber."

"And your theory, Mr. Chambrun?"

"Ah, yes. My theory." Chambrun paused because there was a disturbance behind him. Through the swinging door from the Crystal Room's kitchen came Jerry Dodd, walking briskly, head down. He was followed by Battle, muffled in his overcoat and hat, and Butler and Gaston. They were a few yards in when Jerry stopped, a look of comic surprise on his face.

"Jesus, Mr. Chambrun, I didn't know you were using this room!"

It was so broad I almost laughed. Jerry was lying in his teeth.

Battle gave the reporters a startled look and turned to retreat. There was no place for him to go because Mike Maggio and two bell boys were in the doorway, blocking it with luggage.

"My dear George, I'm so sorry," Chambrun said. "I neglected to tell Jerry we were using this room to see the press."

Jerry looked at me and winked.

"Get me out of here!" Battle said.

"I'm sorry, George, but they'll never let you go. A few answers and I'm sure they won't hold you up long."

Battle looked around him, trapped. His pale eyes fixed on Jerry. "How could you have been so damned stupid!" he said.

"I'm afraid Jerry was just following orders, George. I had to arrange it this way for fear you might have the President himself acting as your guide. They've just asked me what my theory is about how the masked man got into the penthouse. I wonder if what I think will coincide with your thinking, George? You see, I don't think there ever was a masked man in the penthouse."

"I saw him, Pierre! For God sake, he shot at me!" Battle said.

"I'm afraid I don't believe you, George," Chambrun said. "It was a very clever gimmick, but you made your first mistake when you set it up. You wanted to have us all believe that you had been attacked. You got out of your bed, walked over to the bathroom door, fired a shot at the bed's headboard. Then you jumped back into bed and greeted Butler, who came charging in, waving at the bathroom door to indicate the imaginary assassin had escaped."

Battle, somehow, looked stronger and younger, his eyes very bright. "You must be out of your mind, Pierre," he said.

"You planned it cleverly, George, but two things went wrong right at the start. You fired only one shot. That was because, knowing how Butler would react, you had only a second or two to get back into bed. A genuine assassin would have emptied his gun at you. You tried to hint that perhaps the shot had been meant for me, and I think you were afraid I would guess what had happened if I had time to think about it. So you arranged to have me kidnaped. It had two purposes. I would testify that there really was a man in a stocking mask, and I would be much too concerned with my own safety to be thinking clearly about what had really happened here."

"I've never known you to go off half cocked like this, Pierre," Battle said, quite calm. "Hardy searched the penthouse from top to bottom for a gun when he thought the shot might have been fired by one of my people. There wasn't any gun in the penthouse and a gun hadn't been disposed of any other way."

"There was one place Hardy didn't search for a gun," Chambrun said. "On you, George. He didn't search you, naturally, because you were the apparent victim. Incidentally, one thing you counted on didn't happen. Butler, your bodyguard, didn't react the way you expected him to. He didn't see anyone go into your bedroom, but clearly somebody had — if we believed your story, and we did. He didn't understand how it could have happened, but he could have let himself off the hook by saying he'd fallen asleep. The worse that could happen would be a reprimand, you say? Not so, George. These four men who worked for you — Cobb, Allerton, Gaston, Butler — were in an interlocking trap. If one of them betrayed you, all four of them would be thrown to the wolves by you. It was what you held over their heads. Butler did some quick thinking. He had better tell the truth. No one had gone into your bedroom. That way the police wouldn't suddenly pick on one of the others."

I glanced at Butler. His face was the color of ashes. I saw that his right hand was slipped inside his coat, very close to the shoulder holster he wore. I wondered if Chambrun saw that. I noticed that Jerry Dodd was standing very close to Butler. He must be noticing, I thought.

"And what might be the reason for this fancy charade you've imagined, Pierre?" Battle asked.

"You were in danger from two sources, George," Chambrun said.

345

"You were in danger from the film script Cleaves had written. You had to stop that by getting control of it. But you also knew that there were only two people who could have given Cleaves the information he had in that script — Allerton or Cobb. To be safe they both had to be silenced for keeps. To be safe you had to handle it away from your villa in Cannes where an attack on them from outside was impossible. So you came here, prepared to deal with Cleaves — perhaps by buying him off, perhaps by framing him for murder. He would be, of course, a prime suspect when the police learned of his past connection with you. So there are two fake attempts on your life — first by the nonexistent man in the stocking mask, second by the letter bomb. You would make sure the bomb would get rid of one of your enemies, Cobb or Allerton. It would still appear to be an attempt to murder you. You would always have arranged to have one of them open that birthday card for you. The case against

346

Cleaves could be pretty substantial by then."

"An amazing invention," Battle said.

"Not an invention, George. Just something I was very slow to see. My slowness cost Allerton and Cobb their lives. I was puzzled by little things that slowed me down; like how did someone on the outside — because you had to have someone on the outside working for you, George; the Stocking Mask who abducted me, the man who delivered the letters to the hotel — how did someone on the outside know Kranepool's name, which was used to lure me out of my office? You told me how, George, and I didn't pay any attention. You were so pleased with yourself that you told us you hadn't taken the sedatives Dr. Cobb thought he had given you. For a couple of hours Cobb kept people out of your room. We assumed you were out cold. All that time you had access to an outside line. You were giving orders, just yards away from us, to your men on the yacht; your army. As Peter Potter has said more than once, George, nothing in your life is exactly what it seems."

"You think you have evidence that could prove any part of this Arabian Nights' adventure?" Battle asked. "I think I've heard enough, Pierre."

"Not quite enough, George," Chambrun said. "How did Shelda Mason get in trouble with you? Did she catch you emptying Dr. Cobb's oxygen cylinder? Was that when you made it quite clear to her that if she didn't do exactly what you told her that Mark Haskell wouldn't live out the night?"

"A very foolish little girl, but very useful in more ways than one," Battle said. His voice had changed. "I should have known better than to try anything under your nose, Pierre. You haven't lost your touch, it seems. So forgive me if I now become crude." He glanced at Butler. "I think we will leave here now, Pierre, and I think you will not stand in our way unless you want Miss Mason's death on your conscience."

Chambrun smiled a tight, grim smile. "I'm afraid you're a little late, George," he said. He was looking past me, past Battle, to the door at the far end of the room. I looked and my heart jolted against my ribs. Standing in the doorway was Hardy, and with him was Shelda. Shelda!

Butler's gun came out as though it was greased in its holster. "You better stand aside, Hardy. Come on, Mr. Battle."

He started toward Hardy, with Battle right behind him. The room full of people seemed to be frozen. Hardy looked pained, but he, in turn, started toward Butler.

"You better put that away, Buster," he said.

"You effing jerk!" Butler said, and his finger squeezed the trigger.

Nothing happened but a click. He tried again and again. And then, realizing that it wasn't going to work, he swung it at the side of Hardy's head. Hardy caught his arm and broke it across his knee, like a man breaking kindling wood. Butler screamed.

"I forgot to tell you I fixed the firing pin on that gun when I borrowed it for a ballistics test," Hardy said. He looked at Chambrun. "Like you thought, Chambrun, the yacht was a gold mine. Here's Miss Mason, and we found enough evidence to prove that letter bomb was put together on the boat." He glanced at Battle. "Your crew tried their best, friend, but we were a little too good for them. We should, in time, be able to pick out Stocking Mask and your letter carrier."

Battle gave him a mock-courteous bow, and then he turned toward Chambrun. His hands came out of the folds of his overcoat and there was a gun in one of them. The shot went through the ceiling as Jerry Dodd knocked Battle's arm upward with his left. His right struck Battle across the Adam's apple.

And that was that.

Except that Shelda was in my arms, laughing and crying.

I heard Chambrun say: "Any more questions, ladies and gentlemen?"

It seemed there weren't. The ladies and gentlemen of the press were racing for telephones. All except the TV cameraman, who was still taking pictures of the wreckage of George Battle's empire.

THE END

123

Other titles in the
Linford Mystery Library:

A GENTEEL LITTLE MURDER
Philip Daniels

Gilbert had a long-cherished plan to murder his wife. When the polished Edward entered the scene Gilbert's attitude was suddenly changed.

DEATH AT THE WEDDING
Madelaine Duke

Dr. Norah North's search for a killer takes her from a wedding to a private hospital.

MURDER FIRST CLASS
Ron Ellis

Will Detective Chief Inspector Glass find the Post Office robbers before the Executioner gets to them?

A FOOT IN THE GRAVE
Bruce Marshall

About to be imprisoned and tortured in Buenos Aires, John Smith escapes, only to become involved in an aeroplane hijacking.

DEAD TROUBLE
Martin Carroll

Trespassing brought Jennifer Denning more than she bargained for. She was totally unprepared for the violence which was to lie in her path.

HOURS TO KILL
Ursula Curtiss

Margaret went to New Mexico to look after her sick sister's rented house and felt a sharp edge of fear when the absent landlady arrived.

THE DEATH OF ABBE DIDIER
Richard Grayson

Inspector Gautier of the Sûreté investigates three crimes which are strangely connected.

NIGHTMARE TIME
Hugh Pentecost

Have the missing major and his wife met with foul play somewhere in the Beaumont Hotel, or is their disappearance a carefully planned step in an act of treason?

BLOOD WILL OUT
Margaret Carr

Why was the manor house so oddly familiar to Elinor Howard? Who would have guessed that a Sunday School outing could lead to murder?

THE DRACULA MURDERS
Philip Daniels

The Horror Ball was interrupted by a spectral figure who warned the merrymakers they were tampering with the unknown.

THE LADIES
OF LAMBTON GREEN
Liza Shepherd

Why did murdered Robin Colquhoun's picture pose such a threat to the ladies of Lambton Green?

CARNABY
AND THE GAOLBREAKERS
Peter N. Walker

Detective Sergeant James Aloysius Carnaby-King is sent to prison as bait. When he joins in an escape he is thrown headfirst into a vicious murder hunt.

MUD IN HIS EYE
Gerald Hammond

The harbourmaster's body is found mangled beneath Major Smyle's yacht. What is the sinister significance of the illicit oysters?

THE SCAVENGERS
Bill Knox

Among the masses of struggling fish in the *Tecta*'s nets was a larger, darker, ominously motionless form . . . the body of a skin diver.

DEATH IN ARCADY
Stella Phillips

Detective Inspector Matthew Furnival works unofficially with the local police when a brutal murder takes place in a caravan camp.

STORM CENTRE
Douglas Clark

Detective Chief Superintendent Masters, temporarily lecturing in a police staff college, finds there's more to the job than a few weeks relaxation in a rural setting.

THE MANUSCRIPT MURDERS
Roy Harley Lewis

Antiquarian bookseller Matthew Coll, acquires a rare 16th century manuscript. But when the Dutch professor who had discovered the journal is murdered, Coll begins to doubt its authenticity.

SHARENDEL
Margaret Carr

Ruth didn't want all that money. And she didn't want Aunt Cass to die. But at Sharendel things looked different. She began to wonder if she had a split personality.

MURDER TO BURN
Laurie Mantell

Sergeants Steven Arrow and Lance Brendon, of the New Zealand police force, come upon a woman's body in the water. When the dead woman is identified they begin to realise that they are investigating a complex fraud.

YOU CAN HELP ME
Maisie Birmingham

Whilst running the Citizens' Advice Bureau, Kate Weatherley is attacked with no apparent motive. Then the body of one of her clients is found in her room.

DAGGERS DRAWN
Margaret Carr

Stacey Manston was the kind of girl who could take most things in her stride, but three murders were something different . . .

THE MONTMARTRE MURDERS
Richard Grayson

Inspector Gautier of Sûreté investigates the disappearance of artist Théo, the heir to a fortune.

GRIZZLY TRAIL
Gwen Moffat

Miss Pink, alone in the Rockies, helps in a search for missing hikers, solves two cruel murders and has the most terrifying experience of her life when she meets a grizzly bear!

BLINDMAN'S BLUFF
Margaret Carr

Kate Deverill had considered suicide. It was one way out — and preferable to being murdered.

BEGOTTEN MURDER
Martin Carroll

When Susan Phillips joined her aunt on a voyage of 12,000 miles from her home in Melbourne, she little knew their arrival would germinate the seeds of murder planted long ago.

WHO'S THE TARGET?
Margaret Carr

Three people whom Abby could identify as her parents' murderers wanted her dead, but she decided that maybe Jason could have been the target.

THE LOOSE SCREW
Gerald Hammond

After a motor smash, Beau Pepys and his cousin Jacqueline, her fiancé and dotty mother, suspect that someone had prearranged the death of their friend. But who, and why?

CASE WITH THREE HUSBANDS
Margaret Erskine

Was it a ghost of one of Rose Bonner's late husbands that gave her old Aunt Agatha such a terrible shock and then murdered her in her bed?

THE END OF THE RUNNING
Alan Evans

Lang continued to push the men and children on and on. Behind them were the men who were hunting them down, waiting for the first signs of exhaustion before they pounced.

CARNABY AND THE HIJACKERS
Peter N. Walker

When Commander Pigeon assigns Detective Sergeant Carnaby-King to prevent a raid on a bullion-carrying passenger train, he knows that there are traitors in high positions.

TREAD WARILY AT MIDNIGHT
Margaret Carr

If Joanna Morse hadn't been so hasty she wouldn't have been involved in the accident.

TOO BEAUTIFUL TO DIE
Martin Carroll

There was a grave in the churchyard to prove Elizabeth Weston was dead. Alive, she presented a problem. Dead, she could be forgotten. Then, in the eighth year of her death she came back. She was beautiful, but she had to die.

IN COLD PURSUIT
Ursula Curtiss

In Mexico, Mary and her cousin Jenny each encounter strange men, but neither of them realises that one of these men is obsessed with revenge and murder. But which one?